The Atlas
of Anywhere

The Atlas of Anywhere

MARIE BRENNAN

BOOK VIEW CAFE

First published 2025 by Book View Café Publishing Cooperative.
304 S. Jones Blvd. Ste# 2906
Las Vegas, Nevada 89107
http://bookviewcafe.com

Print edition 2025
ISBN 978-1-63632-343-5

"The Şiret Mask" was first published in *Beneath Ceaseless Skies*, November
2017. "At the Sign of the Crow and Quill" was first published in *Lace and
Blade 4*, ed. Deborah J. Ross, February 2018. *Dead Man's Map* was first
published in *Traveling Light: Tales of the Magical Gates*, ed. Worldbuilding for
Masochists, August 2024. "On the Impurity of Dragon-kind" was first
published in *Uncanny Magazine*, July/August 2019. "The City of the Tree"
was first published in *Uncanny Magazine*, September/October 2020. "Silver
Necklace, Golden Ring" was first published in *Uncanny Magazine*,
January/February 2023. "Chrysalis" was first published in *Beneath Ceaseless
Skies*, January 2022. "Never to Behold Again" was first published in *Daily
Science Fiction*, March 2022. "A War of Words" was first published in *Strange
Horizons*, September 2024.

Contents

Foreword

There are five basic schools of thought on the topic of author commentary in a short story collection: 1) put it all together at the front; 2) all together at the back; 3) individually before each story; 4) individually after each story; and 5) don't bother.

For the ebook editions of these collections, I can leverage the format to facilitate multiple approaches, by linking to the notes at the end of each story while collecting the notes themselves at the end of the book. Alas, dead trees are not so flexible, which means I have to pick. You will find all the story notes following the Afterword, and can time your reading of them as you choose.

Because I am a notes-after kind of person myself, for now I will say only that this collection contains eight stories, all of them set in worlds other than our own. They range in length from less than five hundred words to nearly six thousand, and three of them take place in worlds previously featured in other stories and novels of mine. Finally, there is also a poem: the fourth I've published, but the first to be reprinted in one of these collections. I hope you enjoy them!

The Şiret Mask

DANGLING FROM A ROPE two hundred feet above the rooftops of Râu Tare, I find myself questioning the decisions that have led me to this point.

It is abundantly clear to me—far too late to be of any use—that the whole affair is a joke. What makes the Şiret Mask so valuable? Not the gems and precious metals that decorate it; lovely as they are, they pale in comparison to the Ceresc Mask of Lezaur, much less the Zeiţă Mask of the queen, and would not be worth a tenth so much outside of their setting. Not the craftsmanship, either—the mask has been repaired several times, where inferior joins have given way. No one recalls the name of the artisan who made it, so little was she famed; and even the design is unremarkable, being very similar to that used in a hundred other festival masks.

No, what makes the Şiret Mask so valuable is this: that fools like me have dangled two hundred feet above their possible deaths, just for the glory of saying we once had it in our possession.

I'm sure the joke will be very funny later. If I survive the final line.

The chain of decisions that culminated in my acquaintance with that rope is so long that it would be foolish to attempt to recount it all from the beginning. Let us choose as our point of departure a certain afternoon in the parlor of my dear friend Oana, shortly before her brother Codruţ stormed in to interrupt our conversation.

Oana had been an acquaintance of mine in our school days, and I had renewed the connection when I came to Râu Tare the year before. She had helped me find my place in Taral society, and in exchange, I served as her confidante in the matter of her secret lover, the dashing Conte Vântul.

Of course the conte was not her lover in a physical sense. Oana was not so foolish as to throw her future away on a man of such mysterious origins, no matter how much he charmed her. But she assured me that they had pledged their love to one another countless times in the six weeks she had known him, and that he was unquestionably the finest of gentlemen. "You simply must meet him yourself," Oana said earnestly one day in her salon, clasping my hands and gazing into my eyes. "During the Festival of Changes. I trust your judgment, Viorica. If you think well of him, then I will introduce him to Codruţ, and persuade my brother we simply must be wed."

I did not share her optimism. Codruţ was an arrogant and grasping man; he did not let go of his possessions easily, and he counted his sister among that inventory. Had their father still lived, by now Oana would have been married to her sweetheart Nicu, who had adored her since they were children. But Nicu lacked enough money to satisfy Codruţ, and while undoubtedly Oana's conte had the wealth to please him, a mysterious nobleman would threaten Codruţ's sense of control.

On that particular afternoon, however, I had no chance to try and convince Oana of this. Before I had done more than draw breath to speak, the door banged open hard enough to strike the wall. Codruţ stormed through the gap. "It is an outrage!" he announced to the room at large.

Oana and I shot to our feet. "Dear brother, calm down," Oana stammered.

"What is an outrage?" I asked.

In response, Codruţ flung a sheet of paper on the floor in front of me, badly crumpled from being clutched in his fist. I retrieved it, smoothed it out, and held it where Oana and I could both read.

*Before the Festival of Changes is over,
the Şiret Mask will be mine.*

No signature identified this terse message. Only a stamp in vermilion ink: the swirling winds of that infamous master criminal, Laperi.

"He's going to steal the mask?" Oana gasped.

"Over my dead body," Codruţ snarled.

I passed my hand over my face to ward off ill luck. "Of course it will not come to that. Were you not intending to wear the Iavol Mask this year? Your vault is impregnable; with the Şiret Mask safely inside, Laperi's plans will come to nothing."

Codruţ stopped dead in the middle of his pacing. "Leave it in the vault? Absurd!"

"But you cannot possibly risk it!" Oana said. "You spent so much money acquiring the mask—"

He cut her off with a swift chop of his hand. "I would make myself the laughingstock of Râu Tare if I cowered in fear of this criminal Laperi. No, dear sister—I will wear the mask. With a score of my finest guards around me. Let him try for it; I will leave him bleeding in the street."

"You do recall he has an airship full of minions," I reminded Codruţ. Everyone knew of it: the *Vulpea Cerului*, with its black-painted balloon, like a piece of the night sky itself. "He will swoop down on you from above, and his minions will overpower your guards."

"Then I will hire a wizard, too!" Codruţ had the bit in his teeth. "I went to great lengths to acquire the mask, and I will no more hide it away than I will let that bastard take it from me."

This is a sample of the behavior the mask engenders in those who come within its orbit. People have whispered from time to time that the mask itself is enchanted—or perhaps cursed— because they can think of no rational reason why people would go to such lengths to acquire it. They fail to understand that the reason is *not* rational. Men and women of a certain character are bound to crave prestige. The Şiret Mask is a prestigious item; therefore they desire it, and will not let anyone else have it. Human nature, not magic, is the explanation.

Rationality does assert itself in other places, though. Codruţ could not hope to hire a wizard, not for such a venial purpose as guarding his trinket. He was determined to try, though, and soon stormed off to do precisely that. In his wake, Oana sank back into her chair. "Gods of the change! It will serve Codruţ right if he loses that mask. Such a silly thing—he only wanted it because he didn't have it."

I remained where I was, looking at the door Codruţ had slammed behind him. "Oana—darling—"

"Yes, Viorica?"

I bit my lip, then turned and crouched at her feet. "About your Conte Vântul. I…have a terrible suspicion."

She blinked down at me. "Whatever do you mean?"

"Don't you think it's just a little too convenient? He shows up in Râu Tare, and not long after, we have Laperi announcing his plans to steal the mask. The mask your brother is so proud of owning. And you yourself have become so very dear to him in such a short time."

One infinitesimal movement at a time, Oana's look of confusion transformed into disbelief. "You—you cannot be suggesting that he works for Laperi." Another moment passed. "That he *is* Laperi?"

"I am not certain," I hastened to reassure her. "Only… cautious. The Conte Vântul was in Malspre last year, was he not? And so was Laperi, when he filched the Star Sapphire of Avere. Tell me—has your conte ever been to Riazănoapte?"

Her silence was answer enough. And in Riazănoapte, of course, Laperi had stolen the famed Book of Ceannanas.

I took her hands and squeezed them. "It could be coincidence. Or your conte might be hunting Laperi, trying to bring him to justice! But…be careful."

"How can I be careful?" Oana whispered. "You—please, Viorica, you *must* see him for yourself. You will know he cannot possibly be such a man. Or if he is, you will be able to tell, I'm sure of it. And then I will wash my hands of him forever."

Myself and the Conte Vântul, both at the Festival of Changes. Laughing, I said, "It will be a very interesting night."

Word got out, of course. Laperi had announced his plan to steal the mask, and Codruț made no secret of his refusal to keep it hidden away for safety; there was no better fodder for gossip. Half the street plays I passed in the following days were hastily written pieces about the history of the Șiret Mask: how it was buried in a field to protect it when the Keleti invaded and found years later by a farmer with his plow; how a priest had pronounced the mask cursed, as a way of tricking Domn Avutins into surrendering it to his care; how the infamous thief Răsușa had stolen the mask just to prevent her rival from acquiring it; how Doamnă Paniu took a drunken bet to place it on her horse and lost it when the horse bolted. The puppeteers for the horse were quite impressive.

The other half of the street plays were tales of the thief Laperi, and those did not have to be written in haste, for they had been scripted over the years of his infamous career. Singers and actors on every other corner told of his exploits, the treasures he'd stolen and the traps he'd outwitted. In the right parts of the city, I was sure, one could place bets on the outcome of this duel. I wondered how many were betting on Codruț, and doubted the odds favored him…especially after the *Vulpea Cerului* was indeed sighted in the mountains outside the city.

All of this simply added to the chaos that accompanied any Festival of Changes. The celebrations were each person's chance to shed their bad luck, donning a mask so that the gods would lose sight of them. For the city it marked the start of the new year; for the citizens, it was the chance of a new life, even if only for a few hours. Nobles could cast off their responsibilities and commoners speak their minds. The brave and the desperate could even go to a wizard and ask to be changed—to wake up tomorrow a different person entirely.

My own plans were not so ambitious. "Here," I said to Nicu,

under the shadow of the Skewed Arch near the river. I pressed a lover's token into his hand. They were a common symbol of the festival; exchanging them was a sign that the two parties had exchanged hearts. "She'll be at the foot of the Estic Bridge at midnight. Don't be late."

Nicu curled his fingers around the token, an intricate knot of thread. "Are you sure?" he said anxiously. "This Conte Vântul—"

"Will be out of the running long before then," I assured him. "But Oana will need you tonight, Nicu. Don't fail her."

"I won't," he said fervently.

The river was on fire with the light of the setting sun, the Gagiu Bridge stretching its shadow along the water. The Festival would officially begin at sundown, but revelers already crowded the river walk and the bridge itself, and when a figure appeared atop the bridge's central market, one might have thought it simply a drunken fool out to impress his lady-love.

Except that the figure was garbed all in black, his flowing cloak and wide-brimmed hat instantly recognizable. We had seen a dozen actors impersonating him on the streets of Râu Tare.

"Laperi!" Nicu gasped.

The master thief's laugh carried across the sudden hush that fell. "I have thrown down a gauntlet, and Codruţ Deleanu has taken it up! Let him hide behind his guards in the Plaza of Gems; it makes no difference. The Şiret Mask will be mine!"

City guards were already scrambling after Laperi, but they made only slow progress through the crowd. Too many people were shouting and clapping, rather than stepping aside. What did the common Taral citizen care for Codruţ and his mask? They wanted only to be entertained—and Laperi was nothing if not skilled at entertaining his audience. With a swirl of his cloak, he leapt down into the market. I had no doubt that he would be long gone by the time the guards arrived.

"Maybe if I help Codruţ—" Nicu began.

"Help him?" I said with a sniff. "If he loses the mask, it will be no more than he deserves. Help Oana, Nicu. The Estic Bridge at midnight—don't forget."

He touched his fist to his heart. With a pat on his shoulder, I left him and went to find Oana.

Had I not seen Oana's costume before the Festival, I might never have found her in the mass of people that thronged the Plaza of Gold. She was resplendent in costume as a lady of ancient Sarazdat, with a mask in the filigree style that was more a nod in the direction of concealment than an effective shield. There are advantages to being a tall lady looking for another lady of considerable height; I was able to spot her and wend my way to her side.

"Did you see Laperi?" I asked.

Oana fluttered her fan nervously. "I did. But I have not seen the conte."

Her tone made her suspicions more than clear. "I am sure he will be here at any moment," I soothed her. "Shall I fetch you some iced pomegranate wine while we wait? I think I see a vendor over there, and I am parched."

She nodded, distracted, and I slipped away into the crowd.

On an ordinary night, fetching two cups of wine would have been the work of a moment. In the teeming masses of the Festival, one might as well try to fetch the Şiret Mask itself. I returned to Oana's side a good deal later with my hands empty. "I am so sorry," I told her. "I think I chased him halfway across the city, but by the time I caught him, his barrel was empty."

"It does not matter," she said. "The conte was here, and full of apologies for his tardiness. I do not know whether to believe him or not. He could not possibly have been atop the bridge, could he? I cannot imagine that he could have switched from that dreadful black outfit into his costume so rapidly."

"Where is the conte?" I asked, craning my neck. Dancers filled the center of the plaza, close-packed enough that it was a wonder more of them didn't step on trailing hems or snag their jeweled embroidery against someone else's cloak.

Oana scowled. "That shrew Cosmina claimed him for a dance.

I haven't seen him since."

"I am sure he has better taste than to favor Cosmina over you," I said, laughing. "But I will go remove her claws from him, if you like."

"Would you?" Oana said. "I told the conte you would be back soon, but I fear he thinks I've made you up."

"Then I shall teach him otherwise," I said, folding my fan with a decisive snap. "Wish me luck. And if you see the conte before I return, then both of you stay right here, or I may never find you again." With that, I dove once more into the crowd.

What transpired next was less than ideal.

While Oana waited for me to return, hopefully with the Conte Vântul in tow, she kept an eye on the crowd, hoping to see him swirling by in the dance—or better yet, returning to her side of his own free will. And indeed she saw him…but neither dancing with Cosmina or some other lady, nor on his way back to her. Instead he was at the nearby edge of the plaza, slipping into a narrow alley.

I had, of course, told her to stay put. But when her back is up, Oana is no more tractable than Codruţ. And so she followed him.

Two men stood a little way down, their backs to her. One was the conte, in the costume she had seen before: the knee-length cloak of the Cuvântat age on one shoulder, with the curving, crescent-moon horns of his mask rising above his head. The other was a man much more plainly dressed, with a simple cloth domino mask. As Oana crept closer, she heard the conte's familiar tenor—but cold and brisk as she had never heard it before.

"In the Stradă Martescu," the conte said. "Your men are in position and ready?"

"We outnumber him two to one," the man in the domino mask said. "He won't stand a chance. The mask will be yours before midnight."

"Good man," the conte said, and coins winked in the scattered lamplight as they changed hands.

Now, a sensible girl would have crept away and gone to warn her brother. But Oana's passions were up, and she had drunk a little wine; furthermore, she was built like the statue of a Sarazdat goddess, and had often gotten into trouble for brawling when we were in school.

"You *cur!*" she shrieked. The man in the domino mask fled; the conte turned to look. He was just in time to receive Oana's fist to his jaw.

It was an exceedingly stupid way to hit him. His mask protected his entire face; had she struck it any harder, she would have broken her own hand. But she followed this up with a much more effective punch to his gut that sent him staggering back a step, before her inflamed sentiments got the better of her tactics for good. The remainder of her attacks were more flailing than fighting, and he easily caught her wrists to immobilize them.

"I hate you!" she screamed in his face. "You have been manipulating me from the start. I'm done with it! You'll never have the mask. And you'll never have me!" With a swift raise of her knee that tore her skirt, she delivered her final blow, then fled back out into the plaza.

This was the point at which my evening began to spin off its intended path and into the wilds of chance. All I can say is that the gods of the change have their own peculiar senses of humor, and I should have known better than to bait them thus.

I found an archway shadowed enough to shelter me and took off my mask. Oana's blow had cracked it; I would have a bruise underneath, and my other mask covered only the upper part of my face.

The mannerisms of Vântul drained away from me like water, for I had no need of him any longer. Rubbing my jaw and cursing under my breath, I set to work transforming myself once more.

First I yanked off my long cloak and held it temporarily between my knees while I unlaced my other half-mask from my shoulder, where the cloak had concealed it. Then I shrugged out of my jacket and turned it inside out before slipping it back on. The flamboyant cuffs of the conte's outfit went into one concealed pocket designed to enhance the profile of my otherwise flattened bosom; the other I filled with the cloth undermask that had protected my face against the pressure of the conte's formal festival mask. With those in place, I settled the crescent horns around my hips, then let the mask itself hang down as substitute for the bustle I was not wearing. Finally I spun the cloak so its former lining faced outward and tied it around my waist, transmuting it into a skirt covering the horns, the mask, and the boots of the Conte Vântul.

That left me with the light half-mask of Oana's good friend Viorica, and a mark on my jaw it would not cover. I donned it anyway and went back out into the crowd. There were plenty of women out there in the fluttering silk veils of piandel dancers; with a small knife concealed in my hand, it was trivial to snip a suitably colored veil off one of them and drape it from the edges of my mask. Not ideal, but it was the best I could do on short notice, and I could not spare the time for more.

When I was done with this, I saw Oana.

She shouldn't have been there. She should have gone straight to her brother at the Plaza of Gems and told him about the ambush. Instead she was standing alone, a scrap of fabric wrapped about her injured hand, staring into the distance.

When you must hide something, give the observer something else to think about. I rushed up to Oana, veil fluttering. "You have to hide me!"

It jarred her from her thoughts. "What?"

"I heard that Dănuţ Vidraru is going to offer me a lover's token. I've put on this veil so he won't recognize me, but I must get out of—why, Oana, whatever is the matter?"

Sniffling, she told me of the conte's perfidy. "That's dreadful!" I exclaimed. "You must go and tell your brother at once!"

"No," Oana said, flaring up. "He will only mock me for being so silly. I hate them both—and that stupid mask! I wish Codruţ had never bought it!"

If Oana did not warn him, then Codruţ would have no provocation to go to the Stradă Martescu and get into a fight. If he did not get into a fight, then the rest of my plan would swiftly come apart.

I thought rapidly. Could I invite him to dance? No, Codruţ never danced. An ambush elsewhere—but anywhere else would be too public.

I would simply have to improvise.

"Oh, my darling, I am so sorry," I said, hugging her close. My right hand slipped a folded piece of paper into one of the deep pleats around her shoulders. She was forever straightening them; she would find the paper soon enough. "Come with me. I think you need something stronger than pomegranate wine."

Beneath those comforting words, my mind was whirling. I would need a pipe. Some ngimri leaves. A new costume.

And I needed Laperi to keep on distracting everyone.

The order of ceremonies in the Festival of Changes was well-known.

From sundown until shortly before midnight, everyone was free to dance and carouse, to enjoy the liberties of the night. In that final hour, the members of the Consiliu—of which Codruţ was one—would visit a fortune-teller in the small hut constructed at the base of the steps that led to the Temple of Transformation. Everyone visited fortune-tellers during the Festival, but this woman was specially chosen to perform this duty; the fates of such important men could not be left to chance. Codruţ, being the most junior member of the Consiliu, would have his fortune told last.

It was the one point during the festival when he would be alone.

And no one in their right mind would attempt to steal the mask from him during that time. There could be no escape: his guards would ring the hut, and if Codruţ did not emerge with the mask, they would descend with blades drawn. If the *Vulpea Cerului* tried to swoop in, a city airship would catch it before it could rise again. Codruţ was perfectly safe. After that he would be in the temple, and then he would return home, to lock the mask into his vault.

Laperi and his men burst out of a dragon puppet when Codruţ was nearly to the Temple Plaza. There was never any chance of success; there were too many witnesses, too many people who saw a chance to curry favor by capturing so notorious a criminal. It was only by the narrowest of margins that the would-be thieves eluded their hunters and vanished into the night. Codruţ never even had to raise a hand to defend himself. He shouted obscenities at Laperi's fleeing back, and likely would have pursued him were it not for the pressing matter of his duties. His companions recalled him to his task, and they continued onward.

Robed and hooded, I sat in the little hut and did my best for the other members of the Consiliu, as if the real fortune-teller were not in a drugged sleep under the table. I've been a fortune-teller in my time, as need arose, and can be quite good at it when I have cause.

But when Codruţ entered the hut, I was determined not to divine his fate…but to change it.

The sinuous curve of the Şiret Mask gleamed in the candle-light, gold and darkness intertwined. Up close, though, it was less impressive. I could see where the upper part of the curve had been welded back onto the base, and someone had tried to restore the paint on the cheek, but hadn't quite matched the precise shade of midnight blue. It was an ordinary mask, really.

Yet it was also one of the most coveted objects in the world—and tonight it would be *mine*.

Codruţ's step weaved back and forth as he approached my table. I had gone to a great deal of trouble the night before to break into his household shrine and get access to the cloth under-masks stored there. Had Codruţ and his men brawled in the Stradă Martescu as I intended, their sweat and the increased heat of their skin would have activated the chemical mixture soaked into the fabric. After breathing in the result, they would have collapsed in delirium, making them easy to rob. But the night was only warm enough for Codruț to work up a mild sheen of sweat—not enough to do more than put him off-balance.

So I drew a mouthful of ngimri smoke from my borrowed pipe and breathed it into his face.

It worked on him just as it had on the fortune-teller. I caught him before he could fall over and lowered him gently to the floor. Off came my stolen robe, which covered the reversible costume of Viorica Mareșoiu and Conte Vântul. Shed of the skirt and masks, I stripped Codruț of his own garb and put it on. His jacket was much too big for me, even with my own jacket inside; wincing at the waste of fine embroidery, I cut apart my own skirt-cloak and used it to stuff the gaps. I was nearly tall enough; with his cloak over me and the Șiret Mask proclaiming my identity, I should be able to pass muster. The deception only needed to last a short time.

I made sure to wipe down the inside of the mask before I donned it, with Vântul's clean undermask to protect me. The last thing I needed was to lose my own balance along the way.

Then I squared my padded shoulders and went out to join the Consiliu.

There was never any chance that I could make it through the entire ceremony that marked the Festival of Changes. Only members of the Consiliu, a few select clergy, and the temple guards ever attended; I did not know where to stand, what to say, or anything else that might preserve my masquerade. Had I planned this moment well in advance, I might have been able to gather the necessary information…but this was all a last-minute gamble, thrown together when the Stradă Martescu ambush failed. Entering the main chamber, I devoted only a little attention to following the Consiliu members. The rest was on the archway that led to the temple spire.

I had to choose my moment with care. Not too late; if they discovered my ruse, I would find myself with a great many new problems and no solution up my borrowed sleeve. But not too soon, either, or—

Shouting came from behind us.

The question of timing suddenly became very simple. As Codruţ burst into the temple sanctuary, wild-eyed and stripped to his smallclothes, I bolted for the archway.

In a night full of abysmal luck, I could at least thank the gods that everyone was looking toward Codruţ, which gave me a head start. I tore off my stolen cloak as I went and hurled it in the faces of the first guards to follow me up the stairs. The heavy fabric tangled them, and they went down in a painful-sounding heap. I did not stay to watch. Instead I flung myself up the spiraling stairs two or three at a time, cursing the insufficient efficacy of ngimri smoke on men of Codruţ's size.

The bells of the city tolled midnight as I burst out into the open air of the lower gallery. The heavy door would hold off a hundred pursuers, but only if I could find something to block it with, and the walkway around the spire's base was bare stone. With footsteps approaching at speed, I had no choice but to continue fleeing, up the second staircase to the top of the spire itself.

Behind me I heard Codruţ bellow, "You're running out of places to run, bitch!"

He was right. The stairs were so narrow that the padded shoulders of his jacket scraped as I forced myself through the last door, and the lintel nearly knocked the Şiret Mask from my head. Here at least I had no need of anything to wedge it shut; the top gallery was so narrow I could brace my back against the door, planting my feet at the base of the railing that kept me from plummeting to my death.

A moment later something thudded against the panels at my back. It did not trouble me. Codruţ, or whoever was trying to bash the door down, was at a disadvantage: the narrow passage afforded him no good angle of approach or way to build up speed.

He knew it, too. The thudding stopped after a moment, and

a voice began speaking. I couldn't make the words out clearly—they were too muffled by the wood and drowned out by the wind—but I could guess. He thought he had only to wait there until I tired of holding him out, or a city airship came to pluck me from my perch. I could hear a whistle in the plaza below, calling for such an airship even now; that gleam off to my left was one approaching. It would be here soon.

But not soon enough.

The bells of the city began to strike the midnight hour. If *anything* tonight had gone according to plan, then Oana and Nicu were at the Estic Bridge, exchanging lover's tokens. If the gods of the change had any sense of charity, she at least should come out of this happy.

I took a deep breath. A second. A third.

Then I unbraced myself from the door, climbed up onto the railing, and—just as Codruţ threw the door open and lunged to grab my ankle—leapt into the air.

If I die because Codruţ's gloves are too big for me, I will be very, very upset.

My grip is slipping. I'm clutching the rope with everything I've got, but I'm sliding out of the gloves, and I don't dare trust my weight to a single hand for long enough to shake the other one free. Especially not when I'm barely three handspans from the rope's bottom end—I almost missed it entirely. There isn't enough of a tail left for me to catch it between my knees.

I wonder if they'll be able to repair the Şiret Mask after I fall to my death. I suppose it depends on whether I land facedown. The thought shouldn't make me want to giggle, but it does.

The rope starts moving upward. My right hand skins out of the glove, and only a desperate flail renews my acquaintance with the rope before the same thing happens to the left. Now there's only one handspan between me and a swift introduction to the city rooftops passing far underneath my feet. The gloves tumble away into the patchwork of darkness and light below.

But at least my grip is more secure now. I begin climbing as the rope itself drags me upward. Soon I reach the railing, and climb over it onto the deck of the *Vulpea Cerului*.

The Şiret Mask has slipped askew. I untie it from my head, letting the cloth undermask fall to the deck and blow overboard. It can go join the gloves.

My first mate and lover Cserjén claps me on the shoulder. "You made it! Lykos laid a wager that you wouldn't, what with all the last-minute changes to the plan."

"I hope you threw him overboard," I say, catching my breath. "He should know better than to wager against Laperi."

Cserjén tugs off the black cloak and swirls it around my shoulders, where it settles into place like an old friend. More softly, he says, "We almost didn't make it in time. It was a hell of a scramble, getting from the Temple Plaza to the ship, and then up to that spire."

"I knew I could trust you." I lean into his warmth. Being Laperi has gotten easier since Cserjén joined me. He's good at taking people's eyes off me, so I can do things like drug innocent fortune-tellers and take their place.

As Râu Tare recedes in the wake of my airship, I study my prize. Welded and repainted and battered by the years, the Şiret Mask gazes up at me with blank eyes.

Cserjén says quietly, "Was it worth it?"

My layers of masquerade, months of preparation, my final, desperate gamble: all for this. An unremarkable mask, whose only true value lies in the stories told about it.

Stories to which I have just added my own chapter.

I smile at Cserjén. "Absolutely."

At the Sign of the Crow and Quill

EVEN BEFORE Stepan Jedlička slit open the third envelope of his morning post, he knew to dread its contents. The seal told him that his enemy had sent it, and that alone was cause for apprehension. But even with a spike of fear to rouse him from his usual morning stupor, he did not notice the odd stiffness within the paper until it was too late.

Not that noticing would have done him much good. But at least he would have been prepared when something slid free of the envelope and fluttered to the carpet.

It was a feather, and black, and cut at the tip to form a quill. Ink already stained the pale shaft. When Stepan unfolded the letter with trembling fingers, he saw the message the quill had been used to write.

The ninth of Mesjelen.

A simple date. No more was needed: the quill itself made the content of the message plain.

And Stepan must answer. Either concede, and abandon the field to his enemy—or accept, with all the perils that would bring.

He sat like a stone for several long minutes before he bent to retrieve the quill from the carpet. Leaving his breakfast half-eaten, he went into the next room, where ink and a much better pen waited on the desk. The pen he ignored; the ink he uncapped. With many scratches and flecks of displaced ink from the slender crow's feather, he wrote:

Agreed.

Then he snapped the feather in half, laid the pieces and the reply in a fresh envelope, and called for his footman.

The inn that bears the sign of the Crow and Quill stands along the road between Velkoměsto and Rozcestí. The road is well-trafficked, but few of those who traverse it stop at the inn. Only on market days does it see much custom, and even then, other places enjoy far more patronage.

Two things are noteworthy about this inn.

The first is its ownership. The proprietors of the inn are a pair of women, who have handled its business for as long as anyone can remember. Some say they are lovers, which is possible; certainly they share a remarkable closeness, and no man has ever been known to enter their lives beyond the business of the inn. Some say they are sisters, which ought to be unlikely; one woman has skin as pale as the moon and hair as black as the night, while the other is night-skinned and moon-haired. And yet, there is a similarity there that cannot be denied. Others still nod in agreement to both arguments and conclude they are lovers and sisters both, the taboos of civilized society be damned.

The second noteworthy thing is its location. The Crow and Quill stands twenty-one miles from the plaza that marks the center of Velkoměsto, and twenty-six miles from the milestone that performs the same office for Rozcestí. These distances place the inn outside the bounds of either settlement's laws.

Such as the law against dueling.

The sun was out when Stepan departed from his house on the ninth of Mesjelen, and the bright autumn morning seemed like fate's cruel jest against him. He drew the curtains shut and hunched in on himself as his carriage jounced along, slowly at first through the close-knit tangle of the old streets, then more rapidly once they reached the newer outskirts. He could not bear to look on Velkoměsto and think that he might never see it again. Not that Stepan had ever particularly loved the city—not like sweet Evka had—but everything seemed dear to him now, when it might soon be lost forever.

By the time he reached the Crow and Quill, the air had changed. Clouds drew low over the road, threatening rain they did not deliver, and a chill wind thrashed the leafless branches of the trees. The courtyard in front of the stable was empty. Only when the hostler opened the carriage-house doors did Stepan see that another vehicle already occupied the premises.

Even in the dim light of a single lamp, the gilt sigil of Kysely shone bright on the carriage's side.

At least it gave him warning, as the stiffness of the envelope might have done. When he entered the common room of the Crow and Quill, his enemy's presence did not take him by surprise.

Kysely did not see him at first. The man's attention was on the two women of the inn, the ones they called Mistress Vrána and Mistress Pero. As Stepan closed the door behind him, Kysely handed over the broken crow's feather with a flourish.

The night-skinned woman took it with a thoughtful hand. Which one was she? Stepan didn't know. He had never fought any kind of duel before, much less one sealed in this fashion. He'd heard the stories, though. One woman was the Crow; the other, the Quill. Anyone could come to their inn to settle a matter of honor…but for a duel to the death, one needed the mistresses' permission.

He hoped, for one shameful, craven moment, that they might refuse Kysely.

But the dark woman smiled, a thin stretching of her lips, and nodded. Kysely bowed. Then he turned and saw Stepan.

The sight of his enemy's face might as well have turned Stepan to stone. He remained where he was, frozen, as Kysely approached.

"I knew you wouldn't run," Kysely said, with the same careless cruelty that seemed to attend every word from his mouth. "You're too honorable for that, aren't you? Much good may it do you. The time is set: we meet at midnight. Enjoy your final evening—I hear the wine here is acceptable."

Without waiting for Stepan's reply, he turned and vanished up the stairs.

From across the room, Stepan felt the weight of the two women's eyes on him.

Are these two women, Mistress Vrána and Mistress Pero, named for the inn they acquired? Or is the inn named for them?

No one knows. No one can remember when they first came there, and whether the inn stood before their arrival, perhaps under a different sign.

And no one can remember when the crow feather duels began. Men have settled their disputes with one another by means of steel for ages; only recently have laws sought to prohibit this, and failed. Many of these conflicts are settled by the simple drawing of blood. Relatively few are to the death. And of those that are meant to be fatal, only a handful are arranged with a crow's feather quill.

Yet everyone knows the pattern. Make the quill; send the challenge; if accepted, present the broken quill to the mistresses of the inn.

And if there are rumours…well. Of course anything so shrouded in strange ritual will inspire stories. That the crow feather duels are more than mere duels. That the women of the inn are more than mere women. That to win a duel of this sort brings more than simple victory, one man's honor proven over another's dead body.

Not everyone hears the rumours. And of those who do, most laugh them off.

Only a few go so far as to believe, and to sharpen a feather to a quill.

"So," the night-skinned woman said to Stepan, while her pale sister returned to the tap and a waiting patron. "You are the other party in this duel."

Stepan licked his lips with a tongue almost equally dry. "I am."

"And the reason for the duel?"

A hundred thousand reasons. In the end, though, they boiled down to one. "That bastard. Kysely."

She smiled, a thin, carrion-bird smile. "That is always the answer, isn't it? A man you loathe—loathe so much that you cannot bend knee in apology. Not even when you risk death as a consequence."

Stepan welcomed the surge of anger that rose within him. It brought life to his limbs, which were already heavy with the anticipation of his potential demise. "This is not about my pride," he said hotly. "Kysely is a cancer, gnawing away at the king's heart. I have never made any secret of my enmity toward him; on the contrary, I have been honest about it since his first appearance at court. What slanders I have leveled at him are nothing more than the truth. To apologize would be to retract my words, and that I will never do. What love the king still bears for me, with his heart so poisoned against his former allies and friends, I do not know— but I may hope that if Kysely kills me tonight, at least His Majesty's affection for that man will grow cold. And so I may do some good, regardless of the duel's outcome."

The woman cocked her head, studying him. "Is that what you think will happen? Then either you do not know your enemy very well…or you do not know the true meaning of a crow feather duel."

"I know it is to the death."

There was no pity in her gaze. "You should have educated yourself before you came."

The pattern does not end with the challenge, the acceptance, the submission to the mistresses of the inn. But the only ones who see its final steps are those who take part in the duel, and of those, half never have the chance to tell anyone what they have learned.

The women know, of course. They have been doing this for a very long time.

Mistress Vrána makes a small cut in the wrist of each duelist. She is courteous; she cuts the wrist that will not hold the sword, so as not to handicap either man unfairly. The blood she collects in a bowl. The wounds she leaves unbandaged. Then she takes the bowl, with its mingled blood, to her counterpart, Mistress Pero. That one dips a black feather into the blood and writes the names of each combatant in a ledger.

There are many pages in the ledger, and no matter how many names she writes, only half of them are filled.

When the Quill has finished making her record, the Crow moves to stand opposite her and faces the men once more.

"Thus are you bound," the Quill says.

As if in echo, the Crow says, "Kill your enemy—and claim your reward."

Stepan's left wrist burned from the cut, a distraction that threatened to take his focus from Kysely.

His enemy held his blade loosely, its tip carving small, taunting arcs through the air. "Poor fool," Kysely said. "Poor, rational fool. You have no idea what you've walked into. When you die—and you will—I will not simply have proved my honor in the eyes of society. I will have achieved everything I seek. You think you have been my enemy, all this time? You have been my *pawn*. I wanted you to denounce me, to speak against me in public until I had sufficient grounds for this duel. I wanted you to hate me until the thought of apology was unbearable, even when challenged with a black feather. I needed this to happen…and you, my dear pawn, obliged me every step of the way."

Of course Kysely was inclined to gloat. Even now—especially now—his arrogance would not let him stay silent. But his reasons for this duel were insignificant. The only things that mattered now were the swords in their hands, and the blood in their veins. Blood that must spill tonight.

The women stood silent, bracketing the men on either side. Stepan circled, watching Kysely's footwork. The man was an excellent swordsman; lack of skill could not be counted one of his faults. Stepan knew his odds were not good. But still, he—

Stepan's focus wavered again. Before he began circling, the night-skinned woman had been to his right.

She was still there.

Kysely chose that moment to attack.

Stepan retreated in a rush, the world narrowing down to nothing more than his opponent's blade and his own. He blocked two thrusts, three, and then the fourth slipped through, just a tiny graze along his thigh, but it added its fire to the one in his wrist. And when Stepan finally broke free, the night-skinned woman was *still* on his right, the moon-skinned one on his left.

Kysely laughed. "Notice something odd, did you?"

As if to drive the point home, Kysely lunged, causing Stepan to swing clear of his blade. But even as he pivoted, the women did not move in his vision. No matter which way he turned, their positions remained unchanged, bracketing the space of the duel.

Poor, rational fool.

Stepan prided himself on his habit of clear, logical thought. He paid no heed to superstitions—not even enough to remember what they were.

It does not matter, he thought, with the desperation of a man trying to convince himself. All that mattered was the duel, the two swords and the question of who would die tonight.

What came after that would only matter if he survived.

They are not human, the two women who manage the inn on the road between Velkoměsto and Rozcestí.

Most assume the night-skinned woman is the Crow, the moon-skinned one the Quill. It hardly matters; the two are a pair, and never found apart. But the truth is that the pale sister is the Crow, the carrion spirit that oversees the killing and sends the souls onward when they are done. The dark sister is the Quill, the spirit of fate that records their names—and grants the victor his reward.

That is the reason for the crow feather duels, though few know it, and even fewer credit it. Even when duels were commonplace and legal—even when men could commit murder over a question of honor and find themselves applauded by their peers—these confrontations, with all their ritual, had their place.

The defeated party's death is not so much a murder as a sacrifice.

And when the victor pays with so dear a coin, he buys himself a prize that only such spirits can grant.

Stepan's vision swam with pain and exhaustion. His chest heaved, his lungs unable to draw in enough air no matter how much he gasped. His left arm hung useless at his side, and one leg would hardly bear his weight.

Kysely lay dead at his feet.

The sword that had taken his enemy's life slipped from his grasp. It struck the dirt point-first and hung there briefly, swaying, before the weight of the hilt dragged it down.

"Well," Mistress Vrána said. "That was unexpected."

Mistress Pero, her night-skinned partner, stepped forward. "You have killed your enemy. What is your wish?"

Stepan blinked at her, his breath still coming rough and fast. "Wish?"

The pale Crow gestured carelessly at the corpse. "He would have sacrificed your life to gain his ambition. But he lies dead, and you live. Now my sister will rewrite fate for you instead."

The dark Quill flourished her pen, smiling that same carrion-bird smile. "What do you desire? Wealth, power, fame? The love of a beautiful woman?"

Stepan's gut cramped. *Evka.* "You—could you bring my wife back from the dead?"

The Crow laughed. It was a harsh, ugly sound. "Oh, yes. It wouldn't be the first time someone asked."

"Is that what you want?" the Quill asked. Her pen hovered above the ledger.

Stepan opened his mouth to say "yes"…but the word died on his tongue.

Would Evka remember her death? Would she know how she came to live again? How would he explain her return to everyone else? His rational mind spun out a hundred contingencies, details he should append to this wish if he wanted to prevent it from turning against him.

"He's cautious," Mistress Vrána said. She sounded pleased.

Mistress Pero nodded. "But with no need. We do not seek to cheat you. Whatever you ask for you will receive, in the spirit you intended it. If I write your wife's name in my ledger, she will live again, and no one will recall her death—not even you."

But Stepan shook his head.

"Whether I remember or not," he said, "she would not wish it. For her to live again, because I killed a man—Evka would never condone that. I will not dishonor her with my selfishness."

"Then what do you wish?" the Quill asked.

His gaze fell on Kysely's body, and he knew.

"I denounced this man because his influence poisoned the king, and through him, his whole court. I accepted this duel because it was the only way to put a halt to that influence. But you…you can undo it. Make the king as he was before, as if Kysely had never come to Velkoměsto."

Mistress Pero raised one eyebrow. "Only that? An undoing of his influence, and nothing more?"

Stepan made himself stand straight, even though pain whited the edges of his vision when he did. "Only that."

"A noble soul," Mistress Vrána said. She sounded amused.

The Quill simply nodded and wrote a line, then closed her ledger with a clap. No more ceremony than that—and yet, Stepan had no doubt that they had done exactly as he asked.

As her sister bent and picked up Kysely's body, with no visible effort, she told Stepan, "Do not think to someday fight a second crow feather duel. But you are welcome to stay at the inn any time you please."

Stepan retrieved his sword with care, cleaned it with his handkerchief, and sheathed it once more. "Mistresses—I pray with all my heart that I never see either of you again."

Dead Man's Map

IF IT WEREN'T for the sudden, panicked scramble to quarters, the encounter would almost have been funny.

The *Ruffian Queen* had dropped most of her sail as she approached the shore of Nalin, coasting on a steady breeze around its southern headland. Her crew were singing a rousing shanty about the welcoming lads and lasses that were most certainly not going to be awaiting them in the uninhabited cove on the headland's far side. The sun shone down like a gentle blessing, not too hot, the sky decorated with just enough puffs of cloud to look like some sentimental artist's painting.

Then something hove into view around the headland that, though white, was *not* a cloud. It was another ship, coming out of that selfsame cove the *Ruffian Queen* was headed for.

Erilith saw it as soon as her lookout did and had her scope to her eye even as the call came down. What were the odds, two ships practically tripping over each other near an island this obscure?

Low. But a lot higher if the other ship was—

She didn't have to see the whole stern to recognize those lines, the stupidly ostentatious framing around the windows of the captain's cabin. It was a wonder the *Stormwater Moon* didn't sink, with those new carvings weighing down its ass.

"Beat to quarters!"

The words were out of Erilith's mouth before she could think once, let alone twice. She had no desire to take them back, though. Not because it would make her look indecisive in front of her crew. Not because the *Ruffian Queen* had achieved nothing but fruitless hunting for going on three months now.

Because it was the *Stormwater Moon*. And that meant Iretne was on board.

Erilith couldn't spare any time to scan the other vessel's deck for her former lover. The drums had begun rapping out the double-time call that sent the crew flying to the lines and the guns, their bawdy shanty shifting seamlessly into the *Ruffian Queen*'s battle song. Its fierce chorus rang out across the waves; if the *Stormwater Moon* was replying in kind, Erilith couldn't hear it yet.

No, they were too busy bolting. More white bloomed up the *Moon*'s masts, the other ship hastily making additional sail and tacking in an attempt to get away.

"You just try," Erilith muttered through her teeth. Too much of their prey lately had seen the *Queen* coming and rabbited over the horizon before she could set a new bearing and close with them. Oh, she'd taken a few ships, but those all proved to have very little of value on board to begin with. The single one that might have been a tasty prize had been so heavily armed, Erilith had been forced to hole up for emergency repairs before they could even make it here, to Nalin.

Where her crew were supposed to have the time and leisure to make the rest of the repairs. The *Ruffian Queen* wasn't exactly in prime shape for battle. But—the *Stormwater Moon*.

And Iretne. Who by now would have recognized the *Queen*, and Erilith could imagine all too well her reaction. It would look a lot like her pitying, insincere smile the day their captain died and Iretne decided to disrespect his wishes about Erilith taking command after him. "You're just not aggressive enough," Iretne had said cheerfully as she put Erilith over the side after the mutiny. "Whenever you want something, you back off too soon. You do it in battle, and you do it in bed, and you did it here today."

It wasn't to prove Iretne wrong that Erilith was going after the *Stormwater Moon* now. Her crew needed a prize; otherwise, they might begin to desert. But...it wasn't *not* to prove her wrong, either.

Erilith rapped out orders, and sailors swarmed up the rigging to spread additional canvas. She feared it would be too little, too late: of the two vessels, the *Moon* had the shallower draft, and at this tide she might risk the narrow passage between Nalin and the smaller, nameless islet to its south. The *Queen* would have to navigate around, losing precious time.

But the *Moon* didn't make for that gap. She broke for open sea instead…which for Iretne was an uncharacteristic mistake.

Or she can't for some reason, Erilith thought. *Or it's a trap.*

Wood clapped all along the sides of the *Queen* as the gunports snapped open. "Bow chasers free to fire when ready," Erilith said crisply, and her first mate relayed the order forward. A moment later, the guns spoke. The *Moon's* spanker flapped abruptly, and from the burst of splinters below the sail, Erilith guessed a lucky shot had struck its boom. She made a mental note to reward whichever gun crew was responsible; their good aim had cut down on the other ship's maneuverability.

And now the chase was on. Not a sheer test of speed, like the ones the *Queen* had persistently lost in recent months; the islands in this region made the winds too unpredictable for that. Instead it was intricate tacking, dodging shoals and lee shores where they might run aground—and *that* was the kind of contest Erilith and Iretne both relished.

But something was wrong aboard the *Moon*. Even accounting for the broken boom, she simply wasn't moving with the kind of agility and confidence Erilith expected. Passing into the mouth of a wider strait, Erilith saw an opportunity. Bringing the *Queen* up so she presented her port side to the *Moon* provoked an exchange of guns, one her own ship could ill afford in its present state…but it also crowded the other vessel downwind. And when the *Moon* suddenly juddered, her way slowing, Erilith knew her gambit had worked. They'd scraped their hull along the submerged rocks there, springing gods knew how many leaks.

It would be a mistake to think that was the end of them, though. The *Queen* took additional beating as she came around and closed for boarding, every impact making Erilith grit her teeth at the thought of her poor, beleaguered ship. She could see the *Moon's* crew lining up on deck, cutlasses in hand, and from the crow's nests of both vessels the crossbows were doing their best to thin the ranks before hand-to-hand combat began.

Then the gap between them narrowed enough and, bellowing the chorus of battle, the *Ruffian Queen*'s sailors launched themselves across to the other ship.

The melody soon gave way to shouts and percussive steel. Erilith's own boots thudded down on the deck of the *Stormwater Moon*, and she immediately drove aft through the chaos, seeking the helm. By the rules of engagement, if she could get her hand on the ship's wheel, the crew would have to surrender.

Iretne, though…she might well fight to the death before she let Erilith get within breathing distance of that goal. *You back off too soon.* No one had ever accused Iretne of doing the same.

Except that as Erilith kicked a sailor out of her way and flung herself up the ladder to the poop deck, she saw no sign of her former lover.

Only Monthus, who had sided with Iretne in the mutiny five years ago, and who now flung down his cutlass in disgust at the sight of Erilith. "Ah, fuck," he growled. "Fate's spoken; I know when to shut up and listen. The *Stormwater Moon* is yours."

When the explanation finally came, Erilith didn't know whether to laugh or scream in frustration.

Iretne had popped out. Not on purpose, of course; it was one of the few things she feared, vanishing from existence without warning, even though people who popped out always came back eventually. The phenomenon unnerved her—she hated the idea of being at the mercy of things she couldn't control, even though that's what the sea *was*—and Erilith had very considerately not laughed when Iretne admitted her fear.

Her absence left the crew of the *Stormwater Moon* without a captain. Monthus was more loyal than Iretne deserved, Erilith thought with no small amount of venom: elevated to temporary command by her absence, he'd put in at the cove for a few days to see if she would pop back in to her cabin. But when she remained stubbornly missing, he'd seen no choice but to go on with whatever plan the two of them had discussed before her disappearance.

A good decision on his part…right up until he cleared the headland and saw the *Ruffian Queen* bearing down on him.

"Of course it had to be you," he muttered, smacking his heel against the deck of the captain's cabin like he meant to kick through the boards. Monthus was stocky enough that Erilith couldn't discount the possibility. "Bad enough I lost Iretne's ship while she's gone. I had to lose it to *you*."

Her disappearance explained the *Stormwater Moon*'s poor performance during the chase. Monthus didn't have Iretne's deft hand and iron nerve; he didn't dare try to take the ship through the passage that might have let him lose Erilith at the start, couldn't carve a tight enough course through the islets to shed his pursuer. And that enraged Erilith, because she'd finally had a chance to avenge her loss from five years ago, to regain face and prove to her ex-lover that she could go for something and win…only to find Iretne wasn't even *there*.

She couldn't decide whether she hoped that Iretne would pop back in right now, there in her cabin, to see what had become of her ship while she was gone, or that Iretne would pop back in exactly where she'd been when she left, some feet above the open water, and have to race the sharks to shore.

They weren't supposed to ever meet again. Like two hostile cats staking out territory to minimize their fights, they'd divided the waters of the Al'notliri Islands between them. Iretne muscled her way into control of the more lucrative areas, and Erilith made do with the rest.

Why had the *Stormwater Moon* been here in the first place?

Before she could ask Monthus that, a knock came at the door. Erilith yanked it open and found her first mate, Sedivor, outside. "You've taken stock of the cargo?"

Behind her, Monthus barked out a sudden, wild laugh. That combined with the look on Sedivor's face added up to a sum Erilith couldn't read but didn't like. "Aye," the mate said uneasily.

"Some Griastan sculpture, Fjallaniri dyestuffs, a whole lot of Terrekish woodblock prints…"

"Rules of engagement," Monthus said, sounding far too vindictively pleased. "*Stormwater Moon*'s cargo is all yours. *All* of it."

Erilith's jaw tensed. "What else?"

Sedivor stepped back. "I think it's better if you come see."

A Navigator.

A *dead* Navigator.

Standing behind a stack of crates in the hold like the sailors preferred not to have to look at him. Erilith didn't entirely blame them; it was unnerving to have an animated corpse on board. Not that this one was particularly animated—he just stood facing slightly to starboard, lifeless eyes unblinking. Waiting.

This one had been pale even before he died, and now the overlapping circles tattooed to the side of his neck, the Gate symbol of the Navigators, stood out like a bruise. Erilith had seen enough corpses in her time, though, that she wasn't squeamish about touching them. Reaching out, she turned the body around so it faced aft.

As soon as she let go, it shuffled back around to its previous heading.

She stormed back to the captain's cabin. "You're transporting a dead Navigator?"

Monthus shrugged. "It's custom. Gotta help the dead get home."

"How did you wind up with a dead Navigator in the first place? Where did you find him?"

"Jinamy," Monthus said, which was far from a complete answer.

But he didn't owe her answers, did he? She'd laid formal claim to the cargo of the *Stormwater Moon*, and that included the corpse in the hold. Monthus was right; you were supposed to help the dead get home. The dyestuffs and woodblock prints Erilith could sell wherever she pleased—those didn't have to go to their original destinations—but dumping the corpse on some random island… that would be borderline blasphemous.

A blasphemy somebody had probably already committed. Necromancy wasn't an Al'notliri practice, any more than Navigators generally were; someone else must have animated this one, somewhere else in the world where magic like that worked. And animated him to *go home*, apparently, given his persistence in facing a certain way. But why go to that effort, then abandon him in a place that was certainly not his home?

Far too many places lay in the general direction the dead Navigator was facing. For all Erilith knew, she'd have to sail halfway around the world to get him where he belonged. She indulged in a brief, spiteful fantasy wherein Iretne had somehow known she'd encounter the *Ruffian Queen* and had arranged to pop out just in time to stick Erilith with this problem—never mind that popping out didn't work that way at all.

When Erilith closed her eyes, she saw again the rowboat coming in from the vessel offshore. One man working the oars, and one sitting on the bench. Erilith, a mere eight years old, hadn't recognized how unnaturally motionless that second man was; she'd only recognized her father, come home at last.

For the last time.

She opened her eyes. Someone had once gone far out of their way to bring her dead father back where he belonged. Someone, somewhere, might be waiting for this dead Navigator to return.

And if Iretne of all people could be gracious enough to help, Erilith herself would not do less.

She shut the door on Monthus's malicious chuckle and called to her first mate. "We taking the *Stormwater Moon* for our own?" Sedivor asked.

Once upon a time, Erilith would have answered yes before he could even voice the question. After the mutiny, she'd spent a solid year dreaming about proving Iretne wrong, taking back the ship that should have been hers. Now…

Now, Iretne had made it *her* ship instead. Stupid carvings on the stern and all. And more importantly, the *Ruffian Queen* had become Erilith's. She knew every line and spar of that vessel, like they were extensions of her own body.

Claiming the *Moon* for her own would leave the *Queen* to Sedivor. But Erilith knew him, too; he was happier as a loyal first mate than he would ever be as a captain.

"No," Erilith said. "I've made my point, even if Iretne wasn't here to see it. Take the cargo, the powder, and the shot—anything good from their galleys, while you're at it—and cut them loose. We're done with the *Stormwater Moon*."

Arguably, there was no such thing as being rude to an animated corpse. Still, it felt impolite to shove this one in the hold the way Iretne had done—and yet, he couldn't be left standing around in any old place, not when the mere sight of him made even seasoned hands before the mast trip over their own feet with unease.

Still, Erilith wished she could have come up with a better solution than putting him in her own cabin.

She sat, chin propped on her knuckles, and glared at the dead man. Reo, the ship's ocelot, nosed warily at the ragged cuff of the man's trousers and yowled quietly, a strangled sound low in his throat. "I agree," Erilith said wearily, clicking her fingers in a summons Reo naturally ignored. "But what else am I supposed to do?"

Rising, she stared out her stern windows, at the forested shore of Nalin. Much as she wanted the dead Navigator off her ship as soon as possible, it would be foolhardy to put out to sea again without effecting a few more repairs first. And without giving her crew something of a rest, too. The thin crescent of the beach swarmed with people, some clustered around the portable forge, some carrying water from the inland spring, some very obviously trying to look busy so they could stay out in the fresh air a while longer.

Fresh air. The magic that animated the Navigator kept him from rotting, too, but Erilith's imagination refused to stop manufacturing a whiff of carrion for her to enjoy.

She turned back to him, scowling. "This would all be simpler if you could tell me where you're trying to go. And how you wound up on Jinamy. And who's responsible for putting me—you—*both* of us in this mess."

He stood, unblinking and silent.

Pale skin, black hair, hooked nose—but she couldn't assume his appearance said anything about where he'd come from or where he considered home. His clothing was a mishmash of styles, typical for a Navigator. No help there. Nothing in his pockets, either…or if there had been, Iretne had already taken it, and it wasn't eye-catching enough for Erilith to have recognized it as important while looting the *Stormwater Moon*.

Erilith sucked her teeth. Dead bodies didn't bother her, but she hadn't really considered what it would be like to have one standing in her cabin for however long it took to get him home. They were decidedly more unnerving when vertical.

Reo bolted when she opened the door, tail waving like a flag of surrender. Erilith found her quartermaster and got him to supply her with a length of sailcloth; back in her cabin, she approached the dead Navigator, intending to drape him with the heavy canvas and see if that was any better.

Then she stopped, frowning.

In the hold of the *Stormwater Moon*, it had been too dark to look closely at the man, and during the transfer over to the *Ruffian Queen* she'd been too focused on chivvying him into heading in a different direction from the one he wanted. But now she could see that his shirt had been cut open, and then its loose tails roughly shoved back into the waistband of his trousers. *Very* loosely, as if whoever did it had been reluctant to touch the man.

Like the whole enterprise had taken place after he was dead.

Erilith dropped the canvas at her feet and reached for the corpse. "You, uh, don't mind, right? I'm just wondering if you might have a clue under there."

He made no reply, of course. But she felt better for asking—if a touch ridiculous, too.

As delicately as she could, Erilith tugged the fabric of his shirt out and exposed the pallid skin of his chest.

Al'notliri to the bone, Erilith didn't have much use for Navigators. Even the name felt like an insult: *real* navigation meant learning the ways of wind and current, depths and shore. It meant mathematics to understand the movements of the stars, sharp observation to know where one's ship fit into that dance. It took skill and years of training to be a good navigator of that sort.

Whereas this sort of Navigator didn't need anything more than a friend with some sharpened needles and a bottle of ink. Like the others of his kind Erilith had seen, he had a map of the Gate network tattooed across his chest and probably onto his back, an intricate, spidering network branching from node to node. Labels delicately etched below the nodes named off cities, islands, other landmarks—though without the additional commentary some Navigators liked to add, trivial details about restaurants and beautiful scenery.

Had someone cut his shirt open just to look at the map? But that was pointless. The locations of the Gates were well-known. Unless…could he have a record of an unknown Gate somewhere on him?

If so, Erilith was hardly going to be the one to spot it. The Gates had their uses, maybe, but for most practical purposes, you still needed ships and other mundane forms of transportation. She had no particular desire to teleport anywhere if it meant showing up completely naked, bereft of everything that might be useful to her on the other side. As a result, while some people pored over maps of the Gates—usually ones written on objects instead of humans, but not always—and dreamed of where they might go, Erilith only knew the locations of the more famous Gates, and the ones in the Al'notliri Islands.

Which did not include the label tucked under the dead Navigator's left collarbone.

Curiosity and surprise overcoming her standoffishness, Erilith leaned closer to look. There absolutely was not a Gate on Miunte—at least, not that she remembered. There was one on Berit, though, just to the south, which wasn't included in his map.

Carelessness? It hardly seemed likely. Navigators were a cult; they took the mapping of the Gates as a holy duty. But it was true that Gates sometimes vanished from where they'd been, or formed in new locations. Maybe this was an old map? Though Erilith had never heard of a Gate having been on Miunte. And this Navigator, if Erilith was any judge, couldn't be older than thirty.

Unless he'd been standing around dead for a *lot* longer than she'd assumed.

Her gaze swept across his chest, and the more she saw, the more confused she became. It didn't take an expert in Gate mapping to recognize how wrong everything was. The Gates Erilith had heard of weren't marked; others were in locations she knew for sure didn't have them in reality. When she stripped off the Navigator's ruined shirt and his coat, she found the map extended across his back, and so did its errors.

"What the hell is this?" she demanded, despite knowing he wouldn't answer. "Are you not a real Navigator? Just some impostor? But…why?" She could understand Navigators marking themselves with the Gate map, even if she thought the whole enterprise fairly pointless. A *fake* map? That was pointless to the point of incomprehensibility.

Unless it served some other purpose entirely. And as much as she disliked it, Erilith didn't think she could answer that question herself.

So she would have to find someone who could.

Tugging the dead man's coat and shirt back on, she said, "I'm sorry, whoever you are. Getting you home is going to take just a little while longer."

Erilith's crew were far too excited when she told them they were sailing for Griasta. "We're not going to Snail-Lick Island!" she bellowed over the delighted shouts, which promptly sank to disappointed grumbles. "We're going to Rinalre. They may not have hallucinogenic snails, but they'll buy the woodblock prints for a good price, and you all can enjoy a proper shore leave for a few days."

She wanted to leave it at that, but a handful among her crew were clever enough that they'd notice which direction they *weren't* going. "And I can ask a few questions about our dead passenger before we ferry him home. Might even find a ship heading that way who will be happy to take him for us."

"Something wrong with him, captain?" the bosun asked.

Maybe, Erilith thought. "No," she said. "Just a little mystery I want to clear up before we get him off our hands."

This time of year, the winds to Griasta blew strong and steady. They made good time, with not much foul weather to trouble them, and the only bad thing was that Erilith couldn't make up her mind whether it was worse to have the dead man standing in her cabin without the sailcloth over him or with it. She kept placing and removing the drape, and neither option was good.

But it wasn't hard to find a Navigator—a living one—in Rinalre. Griastans rarely chose that life for themselves, but they used the Gates so often to go sightseeing around the world that they made members of the cult very welcome in their lands. Discreet questioning earned Erilith a few odd looks, since everything from her accent to her coat proclaimed her Al'notliri…but it also earned her the name and location of a Navigator she could speak to.

This turned out to be a Pyel individual named Ahcir. They were old and wrinkled and barely came up to Erilith's sternum, but she hoped that—the age, not the lack of height—meant they knew enough to answer her question.

Ahcir's eyes might be half-hidden under the collapsing cliffs of their brows, but the gaze that came through was still sharp. "How many of the Gates did you say are wrong?"

Erilith shrugged. "I have no way of telling. All the ones I know about, but that's admittedly not many."

She felt good about her choice of person to question when Ahcir refrained from making a snide comment about her ignorance. Al'notliri didn't respect Navigators, and many Navigators therefore disrespected them right back. Erilith added, "Could it be fake? I mean—yes, obviously it could. Anybody can tattoo themself with anything they like. What I mean is, if he's a genuine Navigator, would there be some reason he'd mark himself with an incorrect map?"

The shake of Ahcir's head was the most decisive movement she'd yet seen them make. "No. No genuine Navigator would blaspheme like that. I don't merely mean that anyone who would do such a thing is by definition no genuine Navigator; I mean that I cannot conceive of any member of our order doing such a thing. It would defy our entire purpose." They leaned over to peer past Erilith and said, "You didn't bring him?"

"It would have been too difficult to persuade him to leave the ship and come here," Erilith said, gesturing around. Ahcir currently dwelt in one of the many hostels scattered in an arc around Rinalre's Gate. The whole area buzzed with travelers, some of them still wearing the robes and sandals they'd been given when they came through. Erilith could imagine what would happen if she tried to shepherd a corpse through their midst, and it wasn't pretty.

She dug in her coat pocket. "I did bring a list of the Gate names—"

But Ahcir shook their head. "No, the names alone won't be enough. I need to see the network, how they connect to each other."

Fair as that was, it left the two of them in a bind. Drag a dead man through crowds of drunken people looking for a party, or…

Grudgingly, Erilith said, "He's on my ship. You can come look at his map there."

The heavy curtain of their fallen brows twitched in a valiant attempt to lift, but once again, Ahcir forwent the chance to make a comment. Al'notliri captains like Erilith tended not to enjoy having Navigators on their ships. She'd already taken on board a dead one, though; what was a living person compared to that?

"Let me gather a few supplies," Ahcir said, and shuffled slowly away.

✧

At Ahcir's pace, which would have shamed one of Griasta's hallu-cinogenic snails, it took long enough to return to the *Ruffian Queen* that Erilith had plenty of time to question why she'd gotten herself involved in all of this to begin with. She didn't *have* to look under the dead man's shirt. She didn't *have* to come to Rinalre, instead of just sailing him to his final rest. Hell, she didn't have to chase down the *Stormwater Moon* in the first place.

No. That part, she had to do. But the rest…

You back off too soon.

Not this time, she didn't. Her curiosity was up, and if she didn't do her best to satisfy it, the lack would nag at her from now until the end of time.

It was a good thing Erilith's cabin was at the level of the main deck; she didn't think Ahcir could have managed a ladder. Even the plank laid from gunwale to pier was challenge enough that at several points Erilith feared the ancient Navigator would tip over into the drink. But finally they reached the cabin, and Erilith removed sailcloth and shirt alike to reveal the dead man's tattoos.

Ahcir took their time, shuffling in a leisurely circle around him. When they finished the circuit, Erilith asked, "Well? Does any of that make sense to you? Or is he a fake?"

In an uncannily precise echo of their movement earlier, Ahcir shook their head again. "No. This man is—was—a real Navi-gator."

Intrigued despite herself, Erilith asked, "How can you tell?"

But Ahcir didn't answer. Very slowly, they began to drag at the small flat-topped chest in which Erilith kept her private stock of tea. When Erilith realized what they intended, she picked the chest up and set it in front of the dead man. Ahcir accepted a steadying hand as they stepped up onto the chest's sturdy lid, and then at their instruction, Erilith turned the corpse one quarter-turn at a time, while Ahcir copied the fake map onto the paper they'd brought with them.

She bit her tongue through this whole process, but when it was done, she couldn't hold back the question any longer. "So what's the story behind this map? Is it fake? Very old?"

Ahcir began to roll up the paper. "Old? In Fjallanir they'd be most able to answer that question. People there want to record the knowledge of the Navigators."

It was impossible to tell from Ahcir's tone whether they thought such records were a good idea or not. But it hardly mattered. "I'm not sailing to Fjallanir," Erilith said. "I'm already going a long way to get this fellow home, and that would be even more of a detour than this was. But you don't think it's fake?"

The old Navigator lurched down off the chest before Erilith could help and began shuffling toward the door. They got halfway there before Erilith realized they had no intention of answering the question. It only took her three strides to reach the door and station herself in front of it, and unless Ahcir had some weapon or magic trick hidden inside their loose tunic, Erilith was as immovable an obstacle as the Rocks of Dorr.

"You know something," she said, quiet and level. "Something you're not telling me."

Ahcir peered up at her, all tufty brows from this angle. "We don't owe you our secrets, Al'notliri."

Ah, there it was at last: the contempt of the Navigator. Under normal circumstances, Erilith would have let it pass; after all, she didn't care what these cultists thought of her. But she had one of their former comrades in her cabin, along with a growing sense that she'd stumbled into something far larger than one dead man.

A fake map after all? A Navigator somehow gone rogue, and Ahcir didn't want her to know? Otherwise there was no reason not to dismiss it as a foolish bit of decoration. Or possibly old, though Ahcir hadn't confirmed that. Or—

Like a storm wind slapping out of a mild sky, Erilith remembered her own thoughts when she'd first seen that misplaced Al'notliri Gate. That existing Gates sometimes vanished…and new ones sometimes appeared.

Her hands, braced on either side of the door, went slack. "There's no way to know. Is there? If *all* those Gates are new—I mean, if they're ones that will exist in the future—how could you tell? Navigators don't have any way of knowing a new Gate is about to form, do they?"

Ahcir's mouth vanished into its wrinkles, and for a few heart-beats, Erilith thought they would refuse to answer again. That the two of them would stand there, staring at one another, until some-body got bored enough to give up.

Then the ancient Navigator spoke.

"One of the Gates marked on him does exist," they said, gesturing at the dead man, silent and eternally patient. "I heard of it only a few days ago. In Clepoc. Very new."

The man's tattoos were not new. They had the faded look of marks that had been on him for years.

It didn't prove the whole idea. It could be coincidence. Or the grain of truth that made an otherwise elaborate lie look real.

Erilith couldn't quite bring herself to believe that.

Her gaze went to the dead Navigator, marked with a map of the world as it was not…but as it might be.

A world in which the network of Gates was *radically* different. Countries that thrived on the contact with distant locations would find themselves cut off. Lands that currently stood isolated would become hubs. Some of them would welcome it, leveraging their newfound status to gain power on the international stage; others would loathe the influx that brought.

One way or another, the world would change.

"It doesn't happen that often, right?" Erilith said, hearing the unsteadiness in her own voice like it belonged to a stranger. "Even if this is what it might be—decades, surely. Centuries. One Gate at a time."

Ahcir's shoulders lifted far more easily than their brows did. "Maybe."

And maybe not.

Erilith looked at the rolled-up copy in the old Navigator's hand. "What are you going to do with that?"

"We are Navigators," Ahcir said simply. "We keep the know-ledge of the Gates."

"Keep? Or spread?"

She couldn't decide which would be worse: to share this news, or to hide it away. People might do a lot of stupid things if they thought they knew the future, even if they didn't know when that future would arrive. Or if it was even real. On the other hand, if this happened fast, and they were caught unawares…

"I think you should help this fellow get home," Ahcir said. And this time, when they shuffled toward the door, Erilith stepped out of their way.

Erilith didn't think the dead man was heading home.

Maybe he really had lived on the tropical island he led the *Ruffian Queen* to—an island that, from what Erilith could tell, had no inhabitants at the moment. It might have some in the future, though; if she was reading the map marked on his skin correctly, this place would eventually be called Hily, and it would have not one but *two* Gates.

She ordered her crew to stay on board and lowered the dead Navigator in the ship's longboat. Then she rowed him to shore, as someone had once rowed her father, decades ago.

On the beach, he climbed awkwardly out of the boat and started walking. Erilith followed, several paces behind, one hand on her pistol in case it was needed. But that soon fell away, as the corpse took an appallingly direct route up the island's forested slope and Erilith needed both hands to scramble over the rugged terrain. If anyone showed up to threaten her, they could wait until she caught her breath first.

There was no one. Just trees, underbrush, and a steep slope, that terminated in a ridge where Erilith stopped and stared.

In front of her, the ground dropped away again, but now there were no trees. The barren soil and stone ahead formed a broad bowl, and inside that bowl…

The dead man kept walking. She let him go.

She lost sight of him in the steam and foul smoke that wafted through the crater. At one point there was a flare of brightness, which might have been something going up in flames. But no sound.

After she'd waited long enough, Erilith turned and began her descent, back along the trail of trampled grass and broken branches that marked the way she and the dead man had come.

The whole trip took long enough that dusk was closing in by the time she reached the shore. Tired, sweaty, wishing she could strip off and swim in the waves but wanting much more to be far from this island, Erilith rowed herself back across to the *Ruffian Queen*.

Sedivor greeted her as she came over the rail. "He got home okay?" her first mate asked dubiously. "There are people here to give him a funeral?"

"Cremation, I think," Erilith said shortly. "We can set sail."

"Shouldn't we wait for mor—"

"No."

He took it with good grace, recognizing her mood. "Think we can get clear of the reef before dark, all right. Where to?"

It was a fine question. They still had other cargo to sell. Other ships to chase.

Someone, Erilith thought, *cut that man's shirt open. Someone saw that map.*

Someone who might have made a copy—and who wouldn't feel whatever ethical burden Ahcir had about the right way to handle that information. Information that had sent a dead man into the crater of a volcano rather than leave his skin where other people might find it.

Erilith straightened her shoulders. "By now Iretne will have popped back in. Might have even gotten back to her ship. Set sail for Al'notlir. We're going to hunt down the *Stormwater Moon*."

On the Impurity of Dragon-kind

BEFORE I BEGIN, I feel that I should mention the people who made it possible for me to stand before you now. Unfortunately neither my mother nor my father can be here with me today, but my Uncle Matthew and Aunt Bess are, and I thank them both for all their hard work. For most of my life I've been, as they put it, "a little heathen": I've known hardly anything about Scripture, and I only went to assembly at school out of duty. When I turned thirteen my mother was too busy preparing for her work in Akhia to arrange any kind of ceremony or celebration for my passage to adulthood. My aunt and uncle are the ones who noticed that lack, and insisted I come with them to services here at the Langley Square First Nakhonian Assembly-House.

This is a very different place from what I'm used to—I was raised in the Harmonist tradition, inasmuch as I can say I was raised religiously at all—but I have learned a great deal since I began coming here. I particularly have to acknowledge Magister Broughton, who has put so much effort into instructing me these past six months. Little heathen I might have been, but my mother has taught me to respect scholarship, and thanks to the magister I now have a much better understanding of our Segulist faith. I hope I will demonstrate that understanding to all of you today, and especially to him.

Most boys in my position—or rather, most newly-minted young men—choose to discourse upon a familiar subject, such as the origin of our sacred holidays. But as many of you know, my mother is Lady Trent, the dragon naturalist. As such, I find myself drawn instead to a passage from the Book of Priests, on the impurity of dragon-kind.

My apologies, Magister Broughton. I know that isn't the topic you and I discussed when I first told you I wanted to have a proper ceremony for my adulthood. But you told me I should look for a topic that speaks to me, and while I told you at the time that was the Sabbath and its obligations, I've come to realize this one is much more important to me. In fact—although I know nobody expects a fifteen-year-old boy to do original work in any scholarly field, religious or otherwise—I do have an insight I'm eager to share with everyone today. It may not be an answer, but it should at least leave everyone with interesting new questions.

Scripture has a great deal to say on impurity and unclean creatures. Early in the Book of Priests it declares, "This shall be the law for you unto the last generation, to distinguish between pure and impure, clean and unclean, and that you should teach this to all your children." Magister Immanuel Drucker, the founder of the Nakhonian tradition, interprets this as a command to all faithful Segulists, but especially to men of a priestly line. My mother, as Magister Broughton has so often reminded me, is born of such a line, and as her firstborn son, certain responsibilities accrue to me—at least as Nakhonian tradition counts such things. Because of that, and because of my mother's work, I feel a particular obligation to consider these laws closely.

Dragons appear toward the end of the passage that describes which animals are considered pure and impure. In the Revised Samuel translation it says, "These are the animals whose flesh shall not pass your lips, and whose carcasses you shall not touch with any part of your body or any thing belonging to you, because they are unclean; they are an abomination to you, and the *khirosh* with them." I'm afraid six months of study isn't enough to make me fluent in the original Lashon, but I went looking and discovered that most authorities agree the word *khirosh* refers to the dragon commonly known today as the Akhian desert drake. We call it that because of its modern habitat, but other references to the *khirosh* make it clear that such creatures were once widespread throughout southern Anthiope. That makes sense: our early Segulist ancestors were most likely to write about the creatures around them.

The question then is whether the unclean status of the *khirosh* extends to *all* draconic creatures, or only to the Akhian desert drake. To answer this, we have to consider what the reason is for declaring the *khirosh* impure. Is it, as Amos ben Osher suggested, because they "crawl on their legs" but also fly? But as Magister Drucker points out, that passage in the Book of Priests refers specifically to *insects*. Dragons may have six limbs, and sparklings may be small enough that they were once considered insects, but my mother has proved this is not the case. By contrast, Ganix Aritza counts the desert drake among land creatures, because it lairs in caves, and therefore it's impure because it doesn't chew the cud or have any hooves at all, cloven or otherwise. (I have to admit I'm not at all convinced by his argument. I was always taught to be rigorous in my thinking, and I don't think caves are good enough reason to count flying creatures as belonging to the land.) And then Rafal Piotrvich Gomónka says that dragons and other creatures like snakes are unclean because their scaled nature means they belong to the same category as fish, but they don't have fins or live in the water. Apparently he's never heard of coral reef snakes, or other species that *do* live in the water.

I'm familiar with questions like this already because dragon naturalists have similar debates. What counts as a proper dragon, and what doesn't? Most Anthiopean scholars take their cues from Sir Richard Edgeworth, whose book *A Natural History of Dragons* lays out six characteristics required for something to be considered a true dragon: four legs, flight-capable wings, a ruff behind the skull, bones that break down after death, egg-laying, and extraordinary breath such as fire or ice or noxious gas. All of that describes an Akhian desert drake very well, and in fact Edgeworth was a devout Segulist, who was probably thinking about the Book of Priests when he put together his list. But he wrote his book on the basis of travelers' reports and the like: he never saw a living dragon in the flesh, at least not one he would consider to be a *true* dragon.

Magister Broughton probably approves of that. I haven't been able to find out whether Edgeworth came from a priestly line, but as the magister has said over and over again since I began attending assembly here, dragons are impure, and touching their dead bodies—as my mother has done many times—defiles a person.

If Sir Richard Edgeworth is right, and if his criteria match what the writers of the Book of Priests intended, then some draconic creatures may be pure. Bulskoi wyverns, for example, have only two legs and fly, so they're shaped more like birds, and Scripture doesn't list them among the impure birds. On the other hand, they do have scales, so if the issue is that they're conceptually related to fish, then they're unclean.

That doesn't really solve the problem, though, because there are draconic creatures that don't have scales. When I traveled around the world with my mother, she studied a quetzalcoatl in Coyahuac, and that has feathers. It doesn't fly—in fact, it doesn't even have wings—but drakeflies do. My mother was the first Anthiopean to describe those, when she visited the Moulish jungle. They have six limbs, but it's four wings and only two legs, and I haven't been able to find any magister or priest or other Segulist scholar who's rendered an opinion on where those fit into religious categories. Are they birds? Insects? Dragons? Something else? There is no tradition to guide us.

These are difficult questions to answer because our ancestors who wrote the Book of Priests had never seen a drakefly or a quetzalcoatl or even a wyvern—much less things like the dragon turtle I swam with in Va Hing. They didn't write down laws for creatures they didn't know about. And so we have to try to reason out what the Lord intended.

But our ancestors *did* know about sea-serpents. Those appear in the Book of Creation, on the fifth day: "Therefore the Lord made the great serpents of the sea, and countless living beasts, which swarmed upon the earth and in the waters and through the air, in all their various kinds; and He saw that it was good." I spent a whole week reading about that, because magisters and priests have been debating for thousands of years what it means to say that the Lord "saw that it was good" when "all their various kinds" presumably includes the impure beasts as well as the pure ones. There are scholars who say the impure beasts were made at a different time, and others who say that "good" and "pure" aren't the same thing, and so on. I could spend this entire sermon talking about nothing but that, and I still wouldn't get through it all.

Instead I'm going to point out something else, which is that the *molikshim hayam*—translated in the Revised Samuel version as "the great serpents of the sea"—also appear in the Book of Trials, as a sign of blessing on Hazael. He touched the head of one, and Scripture tells us again that this was "good in the eyes of the Lord." Not contaminating at all.

But aren't sea-serpents dragons?

Part of the reason my mother went on that voyage around the world was to look for an answer to that question. Which Magister Broughton very much disapproves of, because she went to many countries where the people aren't Segulist, and do things like eat pig meat. It's true my mother drank a broth made with pig meat—but that was because she was sick, and too delirious to know what she was being fed, and I was too worried she was going to die to ask questions of the doctor, plus I didn't speak Sengtal—

Sorry. That wasn't part of what I planned to say today. I got distracted.

The point is that most magisters and other writers have concluded one of two things: either that sea-serpents aren't dragons and therefore aren't unclean, or that sea-serpents *are* dragons and the phrase *molikshim hayam* should be translated some other way, like "great whales of the sea." But the word *moliksh* is etymologically related to the one for "snake," and the description in the Book of Trials sounds a lot like a sea-serpent. So whales don't seem very likely.

And sea-serpents *are* dragons. My mother is sure of it. She may not be a magister—especially since Nakhonian Assembly-Houses like this one don't allow women to set foot within the house of learning—and she would be the first to agree that she doesn't know much about Scripture, but she knows dragons better than anyone in the world. And her research in Akhia has uncovered something very interesting.

If I tried to explain developmental lability to you in detail, we would be here all day. I promise I will keep this brief, especially since Magister Broughton has gone to such lengths to impress on me the importance of this moment and my responsibilities as the son of a priestly line, which I have neglected for so long. But ours is a faith that prizes learning and intellectual debate, isn't it? Developmental lability is something all scholars going forward will need to grapple with—including Magister Broughton.

What it means is that dragons can change. So can all creatures, through evolution—but with dragons it's faster, and it happens in the egg. The environment they incubate in changes the creature that emerges. Sometimes in bad ways, and they don't survive, but some of them have good mutations, and they survive and pass those mutations along to their offspring.

I can see some of you are frowning in confusion. Let me put it this way, then: you could take the egg of an Akhian desert drake and, within a few generations, turn its offspring into sea serpents.

You could take an unclean creature and turn it into one the Lord considers a blessing.

Sorry—everyone—excuse me—I'm not done yet. I'm sure you'll want to have lots of conversations about this afterward. But I would like to finish first, if I may?

The categories of other creatures may be fixed, more or less; I don't know how long it would take to produce a breed of camel that has a cloven hoof, but it would be a very long time. Longer than Segulism has been around. But draconic species have changed more quickly than that. It's entirely possible—even likely—that the creature referred to as a *khirosh* isn't the same thing as the desert drakes we have today, because the climate of southern Anthiope was different when the Book of Priests was written. And because dragonbone disintegrates after death if you don't preserve it, we don't even have a good fossil record to consult to tell us whether they had two legs or four, scales or feathers, or anything else.

What we do know is this: that the defining characteristic of dragons is developmental lability. Sea-serpents have it, and they are good in the eyes of the Lord. And sea-serpents can be turned into other kinds of dragons.

I won't be here next week, Magister Broughton—nor any week after that—so let me close by addressing a few of the things you're probably going to say then. I imagine you'll talk about impurity and how good things can become polluted, like a person can become polluted by touching the carcass of an unclean animal—the way my mother has done many times in the course of her research. But the Book of Priests says that uncleanness only lasts until evening. It doesn't taint a person forever, even if she's from a priestly line, much less threaten to taint her son if he doesn't repudiate her and all her work. I searched, and I couldn't find anything in Scripture or in the writings of reputable magisters to support that idea.

Also, I think the unique nature of dragons has something very interesting to teach us. The Lord looked upon a creature that is capable of this type of tremendous change, and He saw that it was good. A blessing, even. If I were to go into religious scholarship, I might explore this idea that the Lord approves of change—that He thinks it's a wonderful thing. Changes like women traveling the world and being natural historians instead of staying home their whole lives to raise children.

Ethan ben Shelah once said, "Tradition is the preservation of fire, not the worship of ashes." We Magisterial Segulists may not focus our worship on the literal fire of the Temple in Haggad, but the spiritual fire of our faith still burns within us. At least, it does within me.

Thank you, Uncle Matthew and Aunt Bess, for bringing me here and fanning the spark of that faith. And thank you, Magister Broughton, for teaching me so much—even if the lesson I learned wasn't the one you intended. If you'd like to continue this debate, then you can send your reasoning and references to me, at my mother's address. I look forward to reading them.

A peaceful Sabbath to you all.

The City of the Tree

THE TREE dominated everything. The sky above, the sea below, the earth on which it stood, and the city that sheltered beneath its leaves. Its branches stretched out over the streets and houses of Cahuei, rope-twisted as if by wind, but a century of hurricanes would not have been enough to sculpt the wood of this impossible cypress. Temples and shrines clung to its bark, reachable by rope lifts or, for the truly faithful, a seemingly endless staircase that spiraled up its trunk. Each morning the priestesses greeted the sun from its uppermost reaches and each evening they bid it farewell, their voices fading to nothing before they reached the ground below. The tree had been there since before Cahuei was founded, and its people believed it would be there always.

But now it was dying.

They told themselves they had forgotten none of the old forms, even though no one alive remembered a time before those forms had been outlawed.

They called themselves the Sayacha, the ruling council of Cahuei, and they met between the enormous natural walls formed by the roots of the cypress. The actual council chamber of the Sayacha was long gone; in its place stood the fortress the Jenevein had built. The fortress was both a defense—the Jenevein knew the Issli would never dare to attack them so close to the tree— and a deliberate insult, putting the heart of their military power in a place that used to be sacred, and ought to be still.

None of those who called themselves the Sayacha now were

willing to meet in the fortress.

Six elders gathered, out of the nine clans that made up the Issli. The Fir were nearly extinct, the Pine had no leader they could agree on, and the elder of the Sequoia refused to come. "The Sayacha," she said scathingly when they asked. "That's as dead and gone as the archon of the tree. Call yourselves what you like, but you are not the council of our past. And I am too old to play pretend."

Her words stung, but not enough to stop them. Cahuei was in disarray, freed at last from Jenevein control, but uncertain what to do with its newfound liberty. And while the city hesitated, the tree continued to die.

"We have to cut it down," the elder of the Willow said when the opening rituals were complete. People might only half-remember the songs, but Sutsetu knew the traditional role of his clan; they were the ones to propose swift action.

Swift, but not necessarily ideal. "That's blasphemy," Chimenil said, and on her heels Nazcuc said, "That's *impossible.*"

For the smaller branches, they could do it. But an army of men with axes could not cut through the main limbs: the Jenevein had tried. And even if they succeeded—even if the tree's slow death now made a swifter one possible—the severed material would only fall as a cataclysm on the city below. A city that had suffered cataclysms enough already.

"Restore the rituals," Aptachi said. In past times the Cedar had not been the main advocates of orthodoxy, but one could argue that made their elder the ideal person to suggest a return to the old forms. Year by year, Jenevein laws had strangled Issli traditions; now that those traditions were nearly extinct, looking to the past for guidance was nearly the most unorthodox thing the Issli could do.

Simkitsi gave him a pitying look. "The rituals were meant to placate the archon, to keep him asleep. They won't do any good now that he is gone."

"Do we know that?" Aptachi challenged her. "We only know that he woke after the rituals stopped. Maybe their purpose was to strengthen the tree, and he woke because it began to weaken."

"Or the tree began to weaken because he awoke and *died*—"

They fell to arguing, the elders of the reconstituted and incomplete Sayacha. Which was, in its own way, a tradition as old as the council.

Above them, the tree continued to die.

The danger took some time to manifest. Yes, the archon of the tree was gone, but the tree itself remained, its roots buried deep in the stony headland that guarded the sheltered bay beyond. It had been there forever, and would be there forever; no one gave it a second thought.

Then the leaves began to fall. Their brown, scaly remnants dusted the city's rooftops and streets, the corners where the wind gathered them in drifts. Looking up, one could see the deep, shadow-bright green fading to a duller shade. But mostly people did not look up. They swept their doorsteps and corners, used some of the material for tinder and kindling and threw the rest out, and never spoke of what was happening.

Cahuei was the City of the Tree. For that to end was inconceivable.

The slow fall of dead leaves went on for weeks before the earth shook. Nothing compared to the stone-shattering quakes that had devastated the city when the archon awoke—just an ordinary tremor, such as the region had seen before—but from above came a sound the people of Cahuei would soon learn to dread: the crack of dry wood.

What fell that first time were only a few small branches, limbs that on an ordinary cypress would have been respectably-sized but were mere twigs to the great tree. A handful of houses suffered damage; one person died. The city had faced worse before, and within recent memory.

But it was a warning of things to come.

A storm rolled in from the sea. In an ordinary winter the rain it brought would have been welcome—but it also brought high winds that snapped more branches free. When the skies cleared, the dulled leaves had not regained their hue, and those who claimed the tree only suffered from drought and would soon recover fell silent.

Drought had never touched it before. The tree drew its life from another source, one that had slept beneath its roots for untold ages.

Now that the source was gone. And unless someone found a solution, Cahuei would be the City of the Tree no more.

If it fell, Cahuei might be no more.

At the base of the tree, the argument continued.

"We could pray—"

"To the gods? They grant rich harvests, fat livestock, thick shoals of fish—not life to trees of impossible size."

"We cannot afford to wait for a miracle. We have to take action *now*, before the tree falls and destroys the city."

"A miracle is the only thing we can hope for. Nothing else will save us."

"Yes," Huysiya said. "Only a miracle."

It was the first time she had spoken since the opening rituals concluded. The elder of the Redwood clan was as small as her clan's namesake was tall, a little starling of a woman whose painted wrap had to be pinned to her shoulder to keep it in place. She did not even come up to Aptachi's chin. But she was respected for her wisdom not just by her clan, but by the entire city, and when she spoke, the others fell silent.

Simkitsi was the first to realize what Huysiya meant. True to form, she did not bother to explain to the others, but launched straight into an objection. "We don't even know how."

Chimenil stared at Simkitsi, then at Huysiya. Her hands wrapped tight around her ceremonial staff—one of the few originals to survive, carved out of her clan's redbud and hidden away from the Jenevein conquerors. "Roots of my ancestors. There are stories, a few chants…but even if we manage to piece those together, there's no guarantee we would get what we need!"

"Then we try again," Huysiya said, unmoved. "Again and again, as many times as it takes, until we succeed or the tree dies."

"What are you talking about?" Aptachi demanded. "Try what? How are we supposed to get a miracle?"

A small branch of the cypress, about as large as he was, tumbled from the tree high above. They watched it fall, but could not see where it landed.

Huysiya said, "We must summon a new archon."

They should have known. Wonders like a cypress tree large enough to overshadow an entire city did not happen naturally, and the traditions of Cahuei were permeated with rituals of offering and placation. But given enough time, anything can fade out of memory. If asked, the average citizen might have said, "There used to be something here, yes, but it is long gone."

Not gone. Only sleeping. And when the rituals stopped, so did the sleep.

The people of Cahuei blamed the Jenevein, and not without cause…but if the Issli had remembered the full truth, they might have been able to persuade their new imperial masters to let the rituals continue. Or perhaps not: the Jenevein were known for their arrogance, and might have believed they could turn the archon to their own ends.

But he was ancient, full of power—and free. Whatever human had summoned him from the apeiron, whatever purpose he was originally bound to serve, that had all been lost to memory. No force in the world could bind him now, save his true name, which they did not know.

The people of Cahuei, Jenevein and Issli fighting side by side, were barely able to kill him.

The six elders of the Sayacha did not dare ask publicly for information. To do that would have invited questions, protests, open riot. The Jenevein had outlawed the summoning of archai as a way to protect their own power—but after the destruction wrought by the archon of the tree, there were many who felt that law had been wise.

Instead they worked in secret, as swiftly as they could. Nazcuc's aunt, even older than he was, remembered the chants the people used to sing. *Out of nothing, into the world; out of death, out of the space between deaths, into life and breath we call you.* Those chants were not the ritual; they were the background, the accompaniment, the way the common people involved themselves when their priests and elders undertook to summon an archon. But they were a start.

Chimenil tracked down a rumor of hidden texts, and found none. Instead she found a story that a certain pattern commonly woven into baskets described the path of the dance once performed as part of the ceremony. In recent years the dances of the Jenevein had become more popular, but there were games the children still played which preserved the old steps and gestures—perhaps.

Sutsetu spoke to members of the Willow who had gone into exile and returned after the Jenevein left. Other lands had not forbidden the summoning of archai: spirits from beyond the mortal world, archetypal tales given flesh. Although the rituals used there were closely-guarded secrets, the exiles had heard a few things. Practices drawn from other traditions, whose underlying principles might be extracted from the chaff.

The members of the Sayacha braided together rumor and guesswork and half-faded recollection, fragments left behind after Jenevein control and approximations of things that had never been recorded because the necessary people knew them, and they hoped it would be enough.

They came together at dawn, in the sheltering embrace of the dying tree. They built an altar of all nine woods and hung over it branches from the cypress, both living and dead, bound into sacred bundles with twine. They played drums and flutes. They sang the chants and danced the figures, and prayed, beseeched, *demanded* that something come to answer their call.

From dawn until dusk they called, until they were staggering and exhausted beyond speech, because all the Issli remembered this: that only through trials of endurance could wonders be achieved.

And as the darkness drew tight around them, the air changed. Thickened. Cohered into a body.

A figure like a man knelt on the ground, sand-colored in hair and skin.

They had agreed beforehand. The one who proposed the idea should be the one to act. And—though they did not say it—to bear the glory if this should succeed…and the blame if it failed.

Huysiya lurched forward, shaking from head to toe with weariness and fear. In a voice no louder than the rasp of a dead leaf, she said, "I am Huysiya, elder of the Redwood clan of the Issli, and I bind you to this task: to restore the health of our sacred cypress tree."

The Jenevein used archai all the time. They merely forbade anyone else to do the same.

Their priests knew the art of summoning, as it was practiced in Jeneve. How to call, and how to refine that call, ensuring that whatever came from the apeiron would suit their needs. Not just a warrior, but a defender. Not just a healer, but one with power over plagues. Not just a savant, but a mind that could help them refine the devices they used to maintain their control over conquered lands.

They knew the art of strengthening an archon. When one first emerged from the apeiron, it was invariably weak: lacking in memory, operating on instinct. The Jenevein priests had made a study of how to nurture what they called, observing each archon's aptitudes and giving them opportunities to pursue those, until their abilities flowered enough to be of use—but not enough to break free of the supernatural chains that bound them to serve their summoners.

And they knew the art of dismissing an archon.

Every child understood that when such a creature died, it returned to the apeiron, the formless realm from which it came, there to remain until summoned again. The priests kept a close watch over those they called. If one grew too strong, its power reshaping the world around it, they killed it before it could become a threat.

Then they summoned another to take its place.

Nameless and naked it came from the apeiron. They called it Omastut—the life found in green things—in the hope that the word would prove prophetic. They gave it masculine clothing, because it had male form, and could pass for human for now.

And they asked him how to heal the tree.

"I don't know," Omastut said, laying one hand on the rough, strip-split bark of the cypress.

Aptachi twitched as if he did not know whether to bluster or supplicate. The creature they'd summoned was an archon; he possessed abilities beyond human understanding. But he was also new-summoned, and if Aptachi struck him no one doubted he could knock Omastut down.

"You don't know *yet*," Simkitsi said. "But you will. You do. You must think. Are you a healer? A gardener? Do flowers spring up where you step?"

Her words made them all look reflexively at the ground, even Omastut. The moss beneath his bare feet was unchanged.

Omastut shook his head. "I—I don't know. Don't you understand? I don't *remember* anything. I should know things and I don't. I reach inside and there's nothing there but a hole."

His voice grew strained, half-panicked with absence. The elders thought of an archon as the devastating creature that had woken from beneath the tree, or the imposing figures that had served the leaders of the Jenevein. Not as this: a man scrabbling after the lost essence of himself. He seemed like a man now, not a font of mysterious power.

Not the savior they had prayed for.

Huysiya laid one hand on his arm, bird-light and soothing. "We called for someone to save the tree, and you came. That means you have some way of doing it. It will come to you in time."

The elders of the Sayacha did not say, *Only if we performed the ritual well enough.*

They did not say, *We do not have much time.*

Huysiya knew those things. And if Omastut failed…

The Jenevein were gone. The death of the tree was their fault, but they were not present to take the blame.

The elder of the Redwood was.

No one truly knew the story of the archon of the tree. When he woke his skin was cracked and brown like bark, his hair a trailing mass of scale-like leaves. There was no guessing what people in what corner of the world had originally told his tale, what myth he sprang from, what he might have been like when he was closer to human. They could only know him by how he shaped every-thing around him.

Because an archon could not exist in the world without in-fluencing it. If the story was that a woman had three loyal husbands, three men would in time find themselves gravitating toward her, stepping in to play the roles her tale demanded. If the myth said a man dwelt in a dark forest, trees would spring up to provide him with his proper home.

Not quickly, and not right away. Like a wind growing from a whisper to a gale, archai needed to gain in strength before their presence could exert such force. The man of the forest would seek out a suitable wood long before he caused one to grow around him—as long as he had the freedom to do so.

For the archon of the tree, the people of Cahuei knew only this: that like all archai, he had two aspects, *seimer* and *gemer*, creative and destructive. When he slept he was *seimer*, and the tree grew. When he woke he was *gemer*, and the city nearly fell.

Huysiya took responsibility for Omastut. He could pass for human, and so she lodged him in her home. She fed him the traditional foods of the Issli, even though neither of them was sure if he needed to eat. Frowning as if trying to recall a long-distant memory, he asked if she had foods whose names she did not recognize; when she asked him to describe them, he only shook his head. The words were there, but the knowledge was not.

She took him around Cahuei, from the waterside district of the Reeds to the paved streets built by the Jenevein on the slopes above. She took him around the base of the tree, tracing every gnarled root that gripped the headland like an ancient fist, and the dead branches that littered the ground like bones. She took him up the staircase, ignoring the complaints of her aging joints, around and around the trunk of the tree until they reached the lowest of the mighty branches—and then up farther still, past the shrines the Jenevein had permitted to continue and the ruins of the ones they hadn't, all the way to the highest reaches of the tree, from which it seemed like a person could see to the ends of the earth.

Everywhere she looked, she saw the tree dying.

"Please," she said to him as they sat on the topmost branch that would support them. "I know we have asked the impossible of you—but it is the nature of archai to do the impossible. If you cannot help us, I fear nothing can."

Omastut skimmed his palm along the surface of the branch beneath him. The drying bark peeled up when he tugged at it, a long thin strip, and Huysiya felt like it was a strip of her own skin flayed off.

"Why does this tree matter so much?" he said, measuring the strip between his hands. "It threatens the city below, yes—but that isn't the whole story, is it?"

Huysiya's lips pressed into a bloodless line. One hand, trembling, reached inside her patterned wrap and came out with a little glass vial on a thong. She lifted it from around her neck and passed it to Omastut, who studied it without understanding. "What is this?"

"All that remains of our redwood," she said. "That, and a few other vials like it. The Jenevein burned them all when they decided to break the backs of the clans. Our willow and our oak, our pine and fir and redbud, our cedar, our sequoia, our aspen. And the redwood of my own people."

The ancestral trees of the clans, from which their ceremonial staves had been carved. Staves the Jenevein had also burned, except for three the elders at the time had managed to hide, providing substitutes taken from ordinary branches. "Those trees were the heart and soul of our clans," Huysiya said. "Our sacred places, our reminders of who we were."

"Nine trees," Omastut said, peeling up another strip of bark. "But not the cypress."

"The cypress is the tree of the Issli. It belongs to no clan, and to all of them. So long as we have this, we are still one people; the Jenevein have not broken us. If we lose it—"

She could not finish her sentence. Omastut nodded and tore up a third strip of bark. Huysiya reached out to stop him—then stopped herself instead.

He was rolling the strips of bark into a strand. A strand longer and thicker than the bark itself could possibly account for.

"I don't know how to save your tree," Omastut said. "But there is one thing I can do."

In the lands and among the people where the summoning of archai was openly practiced—places such as Jeneve—they understood there were signs by which an archon might be known. They kept lists of those signs, secret texts controlled and fought over, because they could identify who had been called long before the archai themselves remembered.

They could be used to refine the call itself, increasing the precision of the act.

Some of the signs were marks on the body. These took time to develop, like the bark-cracked skin and leafy hair of the archon of the tree. But others the knowledgeable called icons, and they were objects the archai carried: symbols that represented some facet of their nature, like a warrior's weapon or a ruler's crown.

The elders of the Sayacha had bound their cypress branches with twine and hung them above the altar when they called. And so Omastut, acting on the instinct of his story, had made a rope.

The tree was beginning to split under its own impossible weight. The wound was still small, but it would grow. The pull of the wind and the tremors of the earth would widen it, until the cypress broke in half and crushed the buildings below.

For now, though, the split formed a gap only a little larger than a man. A little larger than Omastut.

"Seven days," he said. "I don't know why seven. Just give me that long."

"To do what?" Huysiya said, mystified.

His hands were still working at the rope. She could not see what he was doing with it. But then he climbed the trunk—she would have sworn it was impossible—and wrapped one end around a small branch just above the split, binding it with a tight knot.

When he dropped down once more, she saw the other end had been shaped into a noose.

"No!" She lunged forward, frail hands out as if they could stop Omastut. "If you kill yourself—"

He would return to the apeiron. They would have to call him again, and all the understanding and strength he had gained, however small it might be, would be lost.

Omastut stopped her with a gentle hand. "I won't die. I'm sure of it. This—" He fell silent, frustrated once more with the void in his mind, created by the endless cycles of death and rebirth. "Think of it as a trial. An ordeal. I will get something from it. Knowledge, I think. And that knowledge may help you."

By hanging on a tree for seven days. It was not a story Huysiya had ever heard—but she had heard stranger ones.

Like a creature that slept beneath the earth for a thousand years, while a cypress large enough to overshadow a city grew above him.

But she was Issli, and she understood that only through trials of endurance could wonders be achieved. And an archon could endure more than any human might hope to.

"Seven days," she said.

"Then cut me down," he said. "And I will tell you what I can. I hope it will do some good."

He took the noose of cypress bark and set it around his neck. As it pulled tight the rope shortened, lifting his body into the air; the split trunk of the tree closed around him until it seemed whole, and only the twist of rope around the branch above showed where he hung.

And the seven days began.

On the first day, the branches stopped falling.

On the second day, the creak of dry wood ceased.

On the third day, dead leaves no longer dusted the city.

On the fourth day, the desiccated green grew shadow-bright once more.

On the fifth day, new leaves began to bud.

On the sixth day, the people of Cahuei breathed freely.

On the seventh day, an impromptu festival filled the streets.

On the eighth day, Huysiya called the elders of the Sayacha together.

"What did you do?" Aptachi demanded, almost laughing in relief. "Where is Omastut? How did he heal the tree?"

"For the safety of the city," Huysiya said, "I will not tell you."

Even in joy, Simkitsi was not without her argumentative side. "What? Why not? If he stays here, he'll start to shape the city around him. We need to protect ourselves against that. We need to—"

"Need to what?" Chimenil said sharply. "Banish him?"

"We cannot," Huysiya said. "Like the archon before him, it is his continued presence that will keep the cypress safe. The tree is part of his story, and so as long as he lives, it must stay alive to play its role."

Silence fell. Now it held only the cry of seabirds and the rush of the wind on which they flew, rather than the slow death cries of the tree. Sutsetu knew Huysiya the best of them all, and knew that within that kindly, delicate body beat a heart that would do anything to protect the Issli.

He said quietly, "Explain."

Huysiya folded her knobbled hands. "He did something to seek out answers—but he could not promise me that when it was done, he would have what we needed. He is young, after all, and not very powerful. But so long as he *continues* seeking, that part of his story will not end. So I left him where he is."

As one, they looked upward. At the towering, rope-twisted branches of the cypress, the one thing the Jenevein couldn't destroy. The tree that belonged to all the Issli equally, and bound them together as one people.

At the price of an archon imprisoned forever.

Huysiya said, "But you are right, Simkitsi. He will shape the city around him, whether he knows it or not. And we do not know what he will shape it into. The only answer, I think, is a counter-balance."

"More archai," Nazcuc breathed.

Conflicting stories, all competing for control of the city. They might have small effects in their immediate vicinity, but none of them would be able to dominate.

Chimenil's voice was cold. "Are we to become the Jenevein, then? Calling them, using them, and killing them when we grow to fear what they've become?"

"No," Huysiya said. "There are free archai in the world. Those who have escaped their bindings, or been released by their summoners. They will know their stories well enough for us to understand what their presence would mean."

A city of *free* archai. There were places where summoning was permitted, and places where it was forbidden, but none of the elders had heard of a place, past or present, where archai were invited to come and dwell.

A city of free archai…and one who was not.

Huysiya said, "If any of you have another solution, I will gladly hear it."

They had lost so much to the Jenevein. Their history, their traditions, and the sacred trees of their ancestors.

They could not lose the cypress.

"Until we find a better answer," Simkitsi said at last. One by one the others echoed her. It had the sound of an oath.

In ancient times the Issli had executed traitors and criminals by hurling them from the headland to the rock-strewn sea below.

Huysiya's body washed up on shore the next morning. She left no message, but the elders of the Sayacha understood. She had passed sentence on herself for her monstrous act—and made certain they would never find where the archon of the tree hung.

Silver Necklace, Golden Ring

"HE TAKES THEM for his servants, and never after are they seen again." That was how the tale used to end, told by grannies at the fire, by performers at the fair.

It always began with a young woman alone, working in the fields or carrying water from the well, on the first day of the absent moon—for it used to be that three days out of the month, that silver circle vanished from the sky. "He cannot enter any house other than his own," the tellers agreed, "but it's no use running, if Nievre comes for you—he's fast as thought and twice as cruel. He'll catch you before you reach safety and take you to his castle of ice, high in the highest mountains. No, there's only one way to save yourself.

"On the spot you must swear a holy oath, never to step under the roof of one who has not fulfilled some condition. But you must make it an impossible condition, for he is both cunning and powerful, and he will try to do what you have named. Forever after that you'll sleep rough, because holy oaths cannot be broken—but better that than to let Nievre take you."

So the story used to go.

She was weeding in the garden when he appeared.

It was the first day of the absent moon, and she knew it—but who could afford to stay inside, idle and afraid? Only the rich, of which she was not one. And she'd been outside on such days before. Nievre was real enough, she had no doubt, but he didn't come for *everyone*. Only one girl each month, all the tales agreed, spread across many lands. A slim risk against a thick certainty of hunger for herself and her brothers, if she let the weeds choke out the potatoes.

A chill wind; a dimming of the sun, though no cloud covered its face. Then he was there.

"I need a servant to care for my house," he said, in a voice as resonant as it was cold. "You will come with me, and after one month I will reward you."

In quiet moments she'd given thought to what she might say, if Nievre ever caught her. One condition after another, each more impossible than the last. Now that the time called for fancy to become reality, this is what stumbled off her tongue:

"By the powers above and below and those in between, I vow I will never step under the roof of one who has not died three times."

Only then did she dare look at him. A tall figure, cloaked and gloved in black, with eyes as pale as frost. Tales of Nievre had been told for centuries; if he was immortal, she reasoned, then he could not die once, much less thrice. And so he could not take her to his castle of ice, high in the highest mountains, to be his servant and never be seen again.

Nievre said, "Then kill me."

Her hands tightened in the dirt. The tellers all said a young woman must name some impossible condition…but had it ever worked? He agreed so readily.

The weed she'd just dug up was mousebane. She had to wear gloves when she rooted it out; women had died for not taking that precaution. Surely for Nievre, it would do.

She offered him the mousebane and said, "Then eat."

He accepted it and ate without hesitation, leaves, roots, and all.

Within moments his breathing tightened to a rasp, and sweat broke out on his face. He collapsed to the ground, and she only just stopped herself from clapping her hands to her mouth—her gloved hands, that had touched the mousebane. As he convulsed, as his face froze into a rictus of pain, she thought, *Powers above and below and those in between, what have I done?*

Then it was over. Nievre lay dead, and he did not rise.

When her brothers came home, they helped her bury him. "Tell no one of this," she said.

The eldest laughed. "Whyever not? Our clever sister has killed a monster out of tales! Surely people will reward you for it."

But she did not want reward. When she closed her eyes she saw Nievre dying in agony, poisoned by her own hand. Monster though he was, the memory haunted her. *What have I done?*

That night she slept outdoors, as she would every night for the rest of her life, because holy oaths could not be broken. In the morning she got up, stiff and numb from more than cold, and went to get water from the stream.

When she turned around, Nievre was there.

"One death I have had," he said. "Kill me again."

His black gloves and pale face were immaculate, as if he'd never been under the ground. She dropped her bucket and snatched out her knife—the knife she'd kept with her the previous night, in case a wild animal troubled her. With a shriek she leapt forward and buried the blade where Nievre's heart should be.

She staggered back. He wrapped one black-gloved hand around the knife's hilt and drew it free. The blood sheathing the steel was as red as any man's. She didn't take the knife when he offered it to her; it tumbled from his hand. Then he staggered, going to one knee, then to the ground. Blood seeped out and sank into the earth, and Nievre stopped breathing.

Even as she screamed for her brothers to come, she knew there was no point.

They buried Nievre again, in ground that showed no sign of having been disturbed.

"We'll stay with you tomorrow," her brothers said. That very night they slept at her sides, wrapped in blankets, weapons at hand, so they would be ready when Nievre came.

None of them had any doubt that he would come.

She was the first to wake, when dawn's light flared across the land. She got up, frozen and afraid—and Nievre was already there.

"They will not stir," he said, before she could make a sound. "This is between the two of us. Two deaths I have had; the time has come for you to give me the third."

Poison had not worked. Neither had a knife. Knowing already that it would do no good, she took up her youngest brother's cudgel and swung it at Nievre's head.

He staggered at the first blow, but didn't fall. She had to swing again—then again, and again, impact shrieking up her arms, even after he'd dropped to the ground, because she couldn't tell if he was dead, because it didn't *matter* if he was dead; he would only come back. She kept beating him with the cudgel, with all the strength of a young woman who worked hard to keep her family fed. Breaking bones, splitting skin. Striking his head again and again until his skull lost all shape and his brains spilled out. She struck until she could strike no more, and the cudgel fell from her exhausted fingers and she sank down next to the unrecognizable mass of red that used to be something that looked like a man.

Horror sobbed in her chest. He wasn't a man. He could die, but it didn't matter. He would take her to his castle of ice, high in the highest mountains; he would take her for his servant, and never after would she be seen again.

When her brothers woke and saw what she had done, they flinched away. They'd vowed to save their sister…but their sister was a sweet girl, not a beast capable of such violence. And besides, she could not be saved.

They didn't bury Nievre. They barely said good-bye. They fled back to their house—her house no more—and left her in the woods one final night.

She didn't think she slept. But somehow darkness became dawn, and the carnage she'd wrought became Nievre once more.

"Three deaths I have had," he said, in his cold, resonant voice.

"I need a servant to care for my house. You will come with me, and after one month I will reward you."

And so she went.

His castle was not wholly built of ice.

It was as cold as the snow, and as imposing as the peak it stood upon. The stone of its walls was black; the panes of its many windows *were* of ice, freezing to the touch. She stood, gripping the silver necklace her brothers had once given her, under the only roof that would accept her now.

Nievre said, "Your job is to maintain this place. Several days you have delayed me; you must work hard to catch up. Begin by sweeping the rooms clean of warmth, and dusting away any brightness that has gathered on the furniture. Tomorrow you can air out the winds." Then he went away, leaving her with her tears frozen on her cheeks.

His castle had many rooms, most of which were unused. He took his meals in a great hall where no fire burned, dining on raw venison and fish; where they came from, she did not know. She had to scrub his plates and his silver clean in water that chilled her hands to the bone. During the day he walked in a garden of bare trees and withered flowers. At night he slept in a bed with a canopy as white as new snow. He did not forbid her entrance into that room, even while he was sleeping: why should he? She already knew what would happen if she killed him.

For her own survival, she ate his leavings and slept in a room small enough for her own body to warm it. No one else lived in the castle. Whatever had become of his previous servants, there was no sign of them now.

But it was not quite true to say she was alone.

She discovered this on the second day, when he set her to air out the winds. Each one had to be shaken out, a vigorous exercise that was the only source of warmth she had in this place, even though the winds themselves were icy. They came in all sizes and kinds, from faint breezes to blustering gales, and some of them, it turned out, would talk.

Her favorite was the playful little zephyr that nipped at her nose and stirred up wisps of fresh snow from the ground. After she'd dealt with the last of the winds—a big, roaring squall strong enough to carry a blizzard on its back—she sat, exhausted, on the castle's front step, and the zephyr blew just enough to cool her cheeks. "You came late," it said. "We thought he might have failed."

"Has it ever happened?" she asked. "Has he ever come home without a servant?"

"Yes," the zephyr said simply. Then it fell quiet while she wept. If she had chosen some other impossible condition—if she hadn't said Nievre must die three times—

But the zephyr had told her the truth, and for that, it became her friend. It didn't stay at her side all the time, knowing she needed to be away from the winds to conserve what warmth she had, but its playful dance was one of her few reasons for joy. After a while she began saving the strands of hair she combed from her head, and gave them to the zephyr to waft here and there. Nievre was angry when he found one on his chair, because her hair was as red as fire, and he did not like such brightness in his halls. "Then he shouldn't have taken *me*," she muttered— though not where he could hear. Nievre was indifferent rather than cruel, but she feared him all the same.

At night she gazed out her window of ice and looked at the stars, at the moon, and her tears froze on her cheeks.

In those days, as I have said, the moon was not like it is now. It hung full in the sky every night except for the three days when it vanished. This made the passing time harder to measure, and so she did not know how long she'd been in Nievre's castle when the zephyr whispered, "Your time is almost up."

She was used to the cold by now, but this chill went deeper. A castle empty of past servants, with only her to care for it. "What do you mean?"

"It is almost time for the absent moon," the zephyr said, its whisper very small. "When that happens, Nievre will go to seek a new servant."

"And what of me?"

Those he took were never seen again. It did not surprise her when the zephyr said, "He will kill you and bury you in the garden."

As she had killed and buried him, more than once. She sank down low, as if that would hide their conversation. "Little wind… how is it that Nievre comes back to life?"

The zephyr shivered. She had not known that it could feel cold—or fear. "His life is not in his body. He's placed it in some possession of his. Whatever you do to his flesh and blood, he'll come back so long as that object is intact."

"Where is it?"

Brightness swirled as the zephyr spun in agitation. She did not always dust her own room as she should, even though she knew it made Nievre angry. What did it matter, if he would kill her regardless? "I don't know," the zephyr said. "Something unliving. Something that was never living. Only that has room in it for someone else's life."

If she'd known this sooner…but Nievre had countless possessions. His life could be in any of them. There wasn't time to destroy them all. He would kill her first.

She said abruptly, "Then I have to hide *my* life."

The zephyr swelled up into a sharp wind. "No! How do you think Nievre got so cold? He used to be human, once. Your life is your warmth. Take that out, and you'll become cold like he is."

"Either I take it out," she said, "or he does. But this way I'll survive. Tell me how it's done."

And, with reluctance, the zephyr did.

The very next night, Nievre summoned her to his room and said, "I tire of your presence. As promised, I shall reward you for your service—with release from it, and from the burden of living."

She stood straight and stiff, trying to hide her fear. "Then kill me."

In his hands he had a length of white silk. He wrapped it around her throat and twisted it tight, and her face flushed dark as air and blood alike cut short. Despite her preparations, despite her resolve, she clawed at his gloved hands, but it did no good. The world pounded and spun and then it went to black, and she fell.

She woke to the zephyr nipping unhappily at her face. "It worked," she said, sitting up.

The zephyr said, "He is digging your grave, and then he will leave to find a new servant."

Down in the garden, Nievre had a shovel in his gloved hands. He stopped mid-strike when she approached, and she took cool satisfaction at the look of shock on his face. He'd never been jarred out of his composure before, not even when she poisoned him, when she stabbed him, when she struck him across the head and he staggered without falling. After a month in his service, that shock felt like wages, long overdue.

"What need have you to seek another servant?" she asked. "You still have me."

"So I do," Nievre said, his gaze sharpening.

He'd looked at her many times. In the field where she weeded; on the path to the stream; in the forest where her brothers lay sleeping. Many times since then, whenever he came to give her orders, the interest draining out of his gaze with every passing day. But now, for the first time, he truly *saw* her.

Nievre laid the shovel on the frost-laced ground. "It seems this is not yet needed. Enjoy your respite. Tonight I will reward you as I promised, and tomorrow I will find a new servant."

She did no work that day. In truth, the castle did not need as much tending as he claimed; it was easier to dust off a few days' worth of brightness at once, rather than scant traces every sunset. That day she walked in the garden, near where he had begun to dig her grave, and Nievre watched her from a window.

At nightfall he summoned her to his room and said, "This time I will do better. By now you must be tired of the burden of your work and the burden of living, so I will release you from them both."

Instead of strangling her, he drowned her. A bath of cold water stood in the corner of his chamber—a bath he had, for once, drawn himself. He forced her head into it, and despite her preparations, despite her resolve, she fought to free herself. To no avail: he was too strong, and the water entered her lungs, and eventually she went still.

"You should run," the zephyr moaned when it woke her the following morning. "Every time you die, a little more warmth slips away. Soon you will be as cold as he is."

"I have no way of leaving this place," she said, sitting up and brushing her frozen hair from her face. "And I will not let him win." He had won the day he came to her brothers' house. Now it was her turn.

Out in the garden, Nievre was digging again, but this time he was facing the gate. He did not look surprised when she appeared, only wary. "Do you not want your reward?"

"I cannot accept a reward from a man who lacks the strength to overcome me," she said, echoing the remote, amused tone she'd heard from him so many times before. She no longer feared his anger, and that gave her a boldness she relished. "Three times I killed you, and three times you came back. Then you had what you wanted. If I come back three times, I should get what *I* want."

"And what is that?"

"I will tell you tomorrow," she said.

She did not wait for him to make more promises or threats. She left the garden and went to sit in a window that gave her a splendid view across the highest mountains, and there she stayed all day.

Until night fell, and she went to his chamber without being summoned, and she found a surprise waiting there.

Nievre had built a fire in the hearth. Branches of one of the dead trees burned, filling the room with heat, shedding brightness over everything it touched. It was the only flame she'd ever seen in the castle.

"Perhaps it will take fire to kill you for good," Nievre said. "If not…"

He did not finish his thought. She reached deep inside herself for the ice that would hide her own. The only unliving thing she'd brought with her when Nievre took her away was her silver necklace. Its links had bit into the skin of her throat when he strangled her; it had dangled cold over her face when he shoved her head into the water. Had he guessed where she'd hidden her life? Could it survive the fire?

Her hands stayed quiet at her sides, not rising to touch the necklace. If he knew, or if the fire was hot enough, she would die. Nothing she could do would change that now.

Nievre was almost gentle as he said, "Come."

She came forward, and she let him push her into the hearth.

This time she did not fight. She did not even scream. She sank down into the flames, and let them take her.

The zephyr did not wake her. The room was quiet and dark—and Nievre was there.

He knelt in front of her as she stepped out of the ashes, clean and unmarked by the flames. In a hushed whisper he spoke, his frost-pale eyes as wide as the sky. "Countless women I have taken from their homes to serve me, and every one of them has died. Not one has come back…except you."

He was a monster, cold as the mountains in which he lived, and he had killed untold numbers.

But not her. She had become as cold as he.

Melting silver takes more than mere hearthfire. Reaching up to her throat, she removed her necklace and offered it to him. "My life is hidden in this chain. Take it, wear it, and be my husband."

His black-gloved hands took the chain and looped it around his own neck. Then, for the first time she'd ever seen, he drew off his gloves. On his left hand there gleamed a single touch of warmth: a golden ring.

He slid it from his finger and offered it to her. "My life is hidden in this ring. Take it, wear it, and be my wife."

Nievre no longer takes a young woman every absent moon to be his servant. Instead his wife Gialle now dwells in his castle, and keeps it clean when she cares to. The rest of the time, it goes untended.

For many long ages Nievre was set in his ways, and sometimes he drifts back. The moon now waxes and wanes with his fidelity, and on the days to either side of the absent moon you can see Gialle's silver necklace, pulling him back to their castle.

She missteps less often. Even so, it happens from time to time. When darkness passes across the face of the sun, a rim of gold appears around the edge, and that is a glimpse of Nievre's ring. It reminds her of his devotion—for what little warmth remains to them is there, in her necklace that he wears, and his ring upon her hand.

But the tales that are told of them now must wait for another day.

Chrysalis

IN FIRE AND THUNDER it was born, vomited up from the guts of the earth in a paroxysm of fury.

Cooled. Broken. Moved. Lost. Buried.

Only for a time. It was a fragment of the divine, and the gods had sent it to the world of mortals for a purpose. It hungered to fulfill that purpose.

Stone is patient. Hidden in its cocoon, the obsidian butterfly waited to become.

The new ground of the milpa stood out like a wound torn into the forest. Without the protective canopy of the trees, the sun blazed hard upon the earth. After the seeds were planted, Konil would have to pile up leaves to keep the soil from being scorched dry, killing the treasure it held.

He'd shared the backbreaking work of clearing this field with the other aluxob of the village. No little alux, no matter how tough-bodied, could cut down and haul away the trees on his own. But now that the milpa was ready, he did the planting alone: pacing off the rows, piercing the ground with his digging stick, burying the red and gold kernels of maize that would feed his family—he hoped. His harvests had been thin for years now, his wife and six daughters reduced to menial work in exchange for seed corn. But the black earth of the new milpa was soft and rich, and perhaps it would yield abundance. Enough to lure a husband for his eldest daughter, who had reached an age for marriage. Then Konil would no longer work alone.

Step, bend, thrust, place, cover. A familiar trance—until his stick hit something hard, just below the surface.

Konil winced at the small shock. Laying aside the stick, he scraped the soil away with his calloused fingers, exploring the thing he'd struck.

A stone. And when his thumb wiped the dirt from its surface, it gleamed.

Konil's breath caught. *Surely not…* He spat onto the stone and wiped again, this time with the kerchief that bound the soft puff of his hair. The barkcloth left behind a smooth, glassy expanse.

"Obsidian," he whispered.

The instant the word escaped his lips, he twisted to look around, as if someone might have heard. But no: he was still alone in the forest, except for the raucous call of a bird, like a warning cry.

Obsidian. The stone was unmistakable; not even the finest flint could mimic its sheen. The local motherfather had a small obsidian knife, shorter than one of Konil's fingers, for use in sacrifices. It had come all the way from Tepatiliztlan, because the priests and nobles of the city controlled the supply and bestowed it according to their will.

Hunching over the stone, Konil searched for its edges. His stubby fingers scrabbled through the soil, burrowing through more and more dirt, heedless of the milpa and his seeds. At last his questing thumb sank past the stone, and a sharp sting told him he'd found an edge. Konil curled his blood-slicked fingers around his prize and pulled carefully.

Soil cascaded as it came up, revealing its full size at last. Konil sank back and laid it across his lap. The oblong was longer than his two outstretched hands laid tip-to-tip. Aluxob had small hands, but still…it was a treasure of unspeakable value.

What strange accident had brought it there? Konil had found stones in his milpas before, but never obsidian. That came from the highlands, many days to the east, where the mountains gave it birth. And such a large piece…

The how and why didn't matter. Only the stone itself mattered, the simple fact of its presence.

It was a gift from the gods.

One for which he'd already shed blood. Konil added a whispered prayer of thanks to his offering. Then he abandoned his digging stick there in the milpa, abandoned his seeds and his water, and hurried home with the stone wrapped in leaves and his barkcloth cape. His wife was out, working in the weaving-house, but he sent his youngest daughter to fetch her, without saying why.

That night they huddled by the soft light of the fire, talking in hushed whispers.

"Great honor, for whoever brings it to the nobles in the city," his wife said. She had refused to touch the stone, but she stared unblinking at its glossy surface, gleaming in the light. "Honor enough to bring husbands for *all* our daughters."

She was right. But Tepatiliztlan lay many days' journey away, and he was a mere alux, a simple farmer who knew nothing of the road. "The trader is here. If we sold it to him—" In exchange for what? Mere cacao beans couldn't fix his family's situation. That would buy him seed corn, yes, but not a fertile field. They needed honor, something to lift them above their low state for good. That meant going to the city himself.

"You must convince the trader to take you with him," his wife said.

She had beautiful eyes, green as new leaves, but tonight the firelight painted them gold, hiding the meaning behind her words. Convince. *Bribe.* But how? The trader was a vay sotz, a creature of the merchant caste. He would drive a hard bargain, and Konil didn't even have cacao beans to pay him with. What offering could they make to the trader that would persuade him to help?

Konil closed his eyes. Perhaps his wife had already seen it. Not cacao beans; not turquoise or gold or carved bone, none of which he had anyway. Something intangible, something even a family as poor as his could offer.

And even the wealthiest of traders might desire.

The obsidian waited on the hearth, cocooned in barkcloth and leaves, holding the promise of the future. But only if they paid its price.

"Chachal," he said at last, opening his eyes. Light flared as a log cracked and the fire leapt up. "She is the only one old enough. And her husband will not care, when he marries the daughter of the alux who found the stone."

His wife did not protest, nor even murmur in shock. She understood the necessity as well as he did.

"Wake her," Konil said. His heart felt like a rock within his chest: not holy obsidian, but common stone, dirty and ugly. "We must take her to see the trader tomorrow. And she deserves to hear the truth before she goes."

Jachanel's people moved swiftly through the forest despite the heavy burdens they carried, balanced on their backs with tumplines across their foreheads to take the weight. Even the little alux farmer carried a basket, despite his small size; no sense wasting a pair of feet, even if he wasn't of the merchant caste.

And after the price Konil had paid for this escort, Jachanel was hardly going to argue over a basket. The daughter was sweet as a berry. Maybe not much of a beauty, compared with the carved jades of Tepatiliztlan, but delightfully modest. She didn't even weep. Jachanel hadn't been cruel; he simply took what her father offered, in fair payment for his aid.

But there was something else about the farmer—something secret. Konil should have known better than to try and hide something from the sharp eyes of a vay sotz. Not for nothing did the lords of the cities hire members of Jachanel's caste as spies. Their merchant duties took them everywhere, and they missed nothing.

The little farmer had hidden something in the bottom of his basket, and Jachanel intended to find out what it was.

When they stopped for the night, Jachanel offered to heat up the atolli. For everyone else he mixed the toasted cornmeal with water and ordinary spices, but the cup he prepared for Konil held something else as well. He carried it to Konil himself and crouched, bringing his lanky height down to the alux's level. "Here. You're not used to walking all day."

Konil accepted the cup gratefully. "I work hard every day. But yes, walking is different. The road hurts my feet."

"It will be worse tomorrow," Jachanel said truthfully. "Get what rest you can tonight."

He would get plenty of rest. The soporific in his atolli was strong, meant for the physicians in Tepatiliztlan; Konil would have slept through the death of the sun. The alux had laid his blanket far from the others—as far as he could get without risking the dangers of the forest—and so Jachanel had both leisure and privacy to unpack his basket.

Most of it was filled with the cargo Jachanel had assigned him to carry. There was a cape and a second loincloth, not much finer than the first, and a small corn-husk doll probably given to him by one of his daughters. But at the very bottom, he found something much heavier, wrapped tight in a barkcloth cocoon.

From the weight alone, his long, bony fingers identified it as stone. Some precious jade? An idol, perhaps? Jachanel pulled back the wrappings, eager to find out.

Obsidian, rough and black as the night around him.

And worth more than Jachanel's entire cargo of cotton and polychrome vases.

In the morning, Konil's blanket was empty. "That's what comes of bringing a farmer among merchants," Jachanel sighed. "They wander off in the night to take a piss, and before they know it, a jaguar has them." Indeed, some of his guards had heard a jaguar in the night. The great cats preferred their prey live, but Jachanel imagined some lazy one had appreciated the easy pickings of a fresh corpse.

It wasn't the first time they'd lost someone during the journey. His bearers shrugged and moved on.

The only inconvenience was that they had to reshuffle their packs to distribute Konil's portion of the load. Jachanel made sure the barkcloth cocoon found its way into his own small pack. Compared to some of the burdens he'd carried, the stone was hardly anything, but he was aware of it with every step he took.

With that stone, Tepatiliztlan's artisans could make one of the great sacrificial knives—not the little slivers villagers used for ritual bloodletting and the slaughter of animals, but something worthy of the great temples and their rites. How great would Jachanel's reward be for delivering such a treasure? He fancied that the stone whispered to him as he walked, promising a great house in the city, with slaves to tend him there, and no more trudging along the trails that joined one flyspeck village to another. It could bring him all that, and more.

But first he had to get it into the hands of the appropriate people.

In Tepatiliztlan Jachanel sold his cargo for cacao beans, instead of trading it for salt and other goods he could carry onward to the next city. Then, with the stone concealed beneath a pack full of beans, he climbed the steps to the palace mound where the priests and the artisans dwelt.

Many guards stood there, low-ranking ocelotlaca adorned with little more than coral and carved bone. "I come to visit an artisan of jade," Jachanel said, and showed a handful of his cacao beans to prove that he could pay.

The guard who had stopped him was female, with broad shoulders beneath her bright fur. The jaguar-woman peered at him suspiciously. "What city were you in last?"

He knew better than to say "Iztlacatun," given all the conflicts between the two domains. "Ohuiyotlan," Jachanel said, thinking it safe—but the name was barely out of his mouth before a powerful, clawed hand clamped down on his shoulder and dragged him out of the entrance plaza, into a smaller room.

The guard ripped the pack from his shoulders and threw him to the floor. Without pausing, she upended the pack, letting out a cascade of cacao beans, and—"No!" Jachanel shouted, but it was too late; the barkcloth bundle fell after them.

It landed atop the beans and rolled. Snarling, the ocelotlacatl tore it open, shredding cloth and leaves alike with her claws. Then she stopped, staring at the gleaming blackness within.

Unharmed, despite its fall. Jachanel let out an unsteady breath of relief.

"So," the jaguar-woman said. "Not a spy from Ohuiyotlan."

Jachanel shook his head, swallowing a curse, and arranged himself on his knees. "I have brought this stone to Tepatiliztlan, so that it may bring the blessings of the gods upon the lord in her struggle against her enemies in Ohuiyotlan." Whatever they had done to earn this kind of suspicion.

A low, rumbling growl came from the guard's deep chest. "A treasure," she said, and her claws tightened around the torn wrappings. Then she sighed. "But one that brings more trouble than it's worth, I think—especially when I have another treasure here. Take your stone, little bat; take it to the motherfather Cenquiztli, and tell anyone who halts you that Nexicolli has said you may pass." She shoved the obsidian back into his pack.

Jachanel took it, trembling, and not entirely understanding. "My cacao beans—"

The golden jaguar eyes gleamed. "*My* cacao beans," Nexicolli said. "Payment for not leaving your entrails on this floor. I could take everything you have, even your life, for lying to me. Be glad I only take your wealth."

He swallowed. An entire cargo's value, scattered across the floor. But he had the stone, and that was worth more than all the rest of it.

"Thank you, noble warrior," he said through his teeth, and slunk out of the room.

Cenquiztli was accustomed to the reactions of strangers. Few understood the decision of the lord to accept a xera within the bounds of the domain, and even fewer agreed with it. The vay sotz trader's narrow, batlike shoulders shrank inward at the sight of Cenquiztli, and he hesitated in the entrance, as if afraid to enter.

"You are safe," Cenquiztli said, with calm patience. "I am the motherfather of this domain, and no danger to you."

One watched the vay sotz advance, unwilling, staring. No mask of flesh concealed one's body; one openly displayed the rough-hewn wooden limbs that marked them as a xera, and—usually—outcast. That was part of one's agreement with the lord. But the shape of that wooden body was Cenquiztli's own doing: on the left side a curved breast and a rounded hip, on the right a broad shoulder and a flat belly. *Motherfather:* a title that recalled the original beings the gods had created, before gender, before caste, before everything. Many people could rise to the rank of that title, but only xera could create, in their own bodies, a shape that echoed that past.

Not easily. The opposition of the seasons touched everyone, but xera more clearly than anyone else. Cenquiztli's form required the perfect balance of spirit: too much of the wet season, and one's body would shift fully male. Too much of the dry, and one would be female.

What the vay sotz brought was a threat to that balance.

"I know what you carry," Cenquiztli said, and watched the vay sotz flinch a second time, his bony fingers tightening around the tattered bundle. "Show it to me."

The trader obeyed, kneeling and unknotting the ties that held the barkcloth tight. "My name is Jachanel. At great risk I have brought this from distant lands, through the domains of our lord's enemies, keeping it safe from their eyes and their hands. I have beggared myself in the process, all so that I might present to the lord this treasure beyond price, this gift to please the gods."

Cenquiztli gazed down upon the scarred blackness of the obsidian. A treasure beyond price: the trader was right. But he did not understand the truth of his own words.

He'd called it a gift. For Jachanel's own sake, Cenquiztli would hold him to that.

"This comes to us in our day of need," one said. "Set it on the floor."

Jachanel obeyed.

"For this gift," Cenquiztli said, "You have the gratitude of the mighty lord of Tepatiliztlan."

The vay sotz waited, but Cenquiztli said no more.

"Motherfather," he began, hesitantly.

"You wish a reward," Cenquiztli said.

"I have beggared myself," Jachanel repeated, and a note of fear entered his voice.

That part of his tale, Cenquiztli believed. He showed the panicked tension of someone who had never imagined walking out of here with nothing.

One knelt in front of the obsidian and raised a four-fingered hand over it, letting it hover like a hummingbird, but not touching. "Of course you have. Obsidian requires sacrifice. When it takes its final shape, it will drink regularly of blood, bearing that most precious substance from the world of flesh into the world of spirit. But for it to transform, it must be nourished."

Cenquiztli looked up, meeting Jachanel's desperate eyes. "I *cannot* reward you," one said. "I cannot give anything belonging to me, of my own free will, nor anything belonging to another—for to do so would be to bind myself within the sacrifices of this stone, as all those who have carried it have done. And that, I *must* not do. I am the motherfather of this domain. You presented the stone as a gift to me and to the lord of Tepatiliztlan; I accept it as such. Your reward must be gratitude, which is not lost by being given. Now go."

Cenquiztli did not watch as Jachanel hesitated, bowed, and departed, leaving one alone in the chamber, without even a fan-bearing slave to stir the air. Let the trader suffer his grief and rage without a witness. What mattered was the stone.

One began to whisper the ritual calendar, the endless cycling of numbers and days, without beginning and without end. Its rhythms were the heartbeat of existence, the footsteps of the sun—which once had stood motionless in the sky, burning all the world to ash, until it was propitiated into motion with blood. Cenquiztli could feel the answering resonance from the stone: obsidian within barkcloth, a cocoon within a cocoon, awaiting its chrysalis.

It was afternoon, and the sun was in a good position. Cenquiztli rose and drew aside the curtain of beads that blocked most of the light from one's small balcony, which overlooked the courtyard where the other high-ranking priests dwelt. The sunlight streamed in, striking the floor and the stone that waited there.

It revealed a striation within the darkness. Rainbow obsidian: Cenquiztli had suspected even before the light confirmed it.

This stone had indeed come to Tepatiliztlan in their day of need. Whatever price it demanded before the end, the lord must pay it. She had no other choice.

Still Cenquiztli did not touch the stone. One's wooden flesh had no blood to give, but the obsidian would claim other things, if given a chance. The wet season was the season of abundance, of giving, of self-sacrifice. The dry season was the season of scarcity, of hunger, of sacrifices taken from others. One had struggled for many long years before achieving the balance one had now, a balance that freed one from the dangers that came with being xera.

That balance might survive contact with the stone. One might be the single person in this domain who could claim it without paying its price.

Or one might not.

I will not try to cheat the gods. Everything in the world came with a cost, from cycle of day and night, to the fertility of the earth, to victory in the wars that threatened to destroy Tepatiliztlan.

The stone must continue on its journey.

Cenquiztli rang a bell to summon a servant. When the young amantecatl page entered, one said, "Send a message to the House of Flint."

Of all the amanteca within the House of Flint, only two truly had enough skill to work a large piece of rainbow obsidian—and from the moment she saw the stone on the floor of Cenquiztli's chamber, Xamania had no intention of allowing Iyaotl to win that honor.

The amanteca were given four days to bring their best pieces before the chief artisan. After studying those, the chief artisan would choose who had the skill to work the stone. The day before the presentation, when Iyaotl left her workroom to fetch water, Xamania slipped in and found the piece her rival had been working on since before the rainbow obsidian arrived: an eccentric flint half as tall as she was, wrought in strange and grotesque branches, with faces chipped into the edges that masterfully evoked the iconography of the gods.

It was almost complete, and finding the right spot took Xamania several breathless moments. She could not shatter the flint; that would be far too obvious. She had to be more subtle. But eventually her clever fingers found an area of thickness, left to support the weight of the branching edges of the flint above. Xamania took out her favorite antler nub and pressed it against the edge, until a shard flaked off. This she snatched up and tucked into her pouch, along with the antler, then replaced the flint where it had been.

Later that afternoon, a scream echoed through the House of Flint. Xamania stayed in her own workroom, imagining for herself the expression on Iyaotl's stupid monkey face when she went to put the finishing touches on her flint and snapped the entire piece in half.

The next morning, the chief artisan surveyed their works, from the clumsy spear-heads of the apprentices to the flawless ripple-flaked blade Xamania presented. Of course he awarded the rainbow obsidian to her.

The tear-stained Iyaotl did not even attend.

Cenquiztli had performed the divinations of the ritual calendar and recommended the day Six Deer as an auspicious time to begin. That gave Xamania four days to prepare, and twenty-one days in which to do the work, ending on One Yellow. She began by cleansing herself and her workroom both, fasting and abstaining from all contact. She'd worked obsidian before—small pieces, shards and scraps begged from the highland cities—but never something of this size and significance. The motherfather had authority over all the ritual surrounding the stone, but the work-ing of it would be hers alone.

On the morning of Six Deer, as the light poured in through the unshuttered eastern window, Xamania settled onto her mat and unwrapped the stone.

Alone in her workroom, with no eyes watching, she found herself trembling with nerves. She held the stone up to the light and observed the colors along its edges, but even the sun's power could not penetrate its dark depths. What waited for her there? Hidden flaws, perhaps, that would snap the core when she struck it, just as Iyaotl's eccentric flint had snapped. Bubbles and imperfections throughout, so that instead of breaking into clean flakes, it would send a shower of useless splinters to the floor. Obsidian was brittle; there would be no using the hard hammer-stones employed on flint and heavy basalt. Antler only, and a great deal of pressure flaking—and if she was both lucky and skilled, the residue of this stone, the pieces chipped free from the core, could be used to make dozens of smaller knives. After years of war and strangled trade, Tepatiliztlan starved of the obsidian supply—starved of its means of speaking with the gods—this could be bounty enough for the entire domain.

If she did not ruin it.

For twenty-one days Xamania worked, consuming only thin atolli flavored with honey after the sun went down, drinking only weak pulque while she worked. She dropped beads of copal incense on the brazier, inhaling the pungent fumes, and prayed to all the necessary gods. Each Day Lord in turn; the patron of the artisan caste; the goddess of sacrifice herself, the Obsidian Butterfly. Each night, when she slept, her dreams were filled with the glassy touch of stone, the pressure of antler against an edge, and each morning she woke to the joy of her work.

Until the sun rose on One Yellow and Xamania held the obsidian up to the window once more. This time she saw its full glory: translucent bands of green and blue, red and gold, the stone flaked so impossibly thin that it seemed hardly to be stone at all.

Xamania would have wept, but tears were not the sacrifice ritual demanded. Instead she took a shard she had saved, a slender point shaded with the colors of the rising sun, and pierced her tongue. Ordinarily she would have caught the blood on bark-paper and burnt it, but this time she let the drops fall, spattering both sides of the blade, down at one end where she had left a neck for hafting. Then, with the copper of her own blood still sharp in her mouth, she took the hilt that had been delivered while she slept, bone inlaid with gold, and bound it onto the blade.

Her work was complete. She had done what no other artisan in Tepatiliztlan had done—might *never* do. Stone for a blade like this came once in a lifetime, if that. Never again would others speak of Iyaotl and Xamania in the same breath, as the two jewels of the House of Flint; now it would be Xamania alone, the pre-eminent artisan of all the city. The chief artisan was old, too. It might not be long before she was elevated to his place, the first flint-worker to be so honored.

No. Not a flint-worker. A worker of obsidian.

Gathering up her triumph, Xamania opened the door, and went to meet her glory.

Motzaloa gazed out over the great nobles of her realm, gathered in her hall to see the blade presented. Tall ocelotlaca warriors; the slender, monkey-like forms of the amanteca; even those few from the common castes who had risen to great office under Motzaloa's rule. But the highest of their finery looked cheap, for the wealth of Tepatiliztlan lay in salt, not gold, and the conflicts with Iztlacatun and Ohuiyotlan had beggared their domain. Even Motzaloa was splendid only by comparison.

She needed a great victory. And to win that, she needed the aid of the gods.

"Master of the House of the Dawn," Xamania said, addressing her words to the stone of the floor on which she lay prostrate. "I bring you the treasure of my hands, crafted with all the skill for which Tepatiliztlan is renowned. May it serve you well."

On the mat before Motzaloa, the blade waited, wrapped in fine white cotton. All the nobles were watching; she allowed herself to betray no hesitation as she reached out and lifted the bundle. It weighed surprisingly little in her scaled hands, scarcely more than the weight of the cloth itself. As if the blade inside hovered, ready to take wing.

And it would, soon enough. But first, Motzaloa would have to make a choice.

She waved Xamania off, watching only long enough to be sure the chief artisan escorted her away. Cenquiztli had spoken to both the chief artisan and Motzaloa; enough time had passed since a great blade was crafted in Tepatiliztlan that only the motherfather knew the rites that should accompany it. Any person who had poured so much of herself into a great crafting could not be permitted to sully that sacred effort with anything lesser. Tonight the chief artisan would shatter the delicate bones of Xamania's hands. She would live on royal largesse for the rest of her life, in remembrance of the sacrifice she had made for her work.

Motzaloa spoke into the silence of the chamber. "In seven days," she said, "at noon on Eight Bird, we shall gather to beg the gods for strength in war. With this priceless blade we shall send a message into the world of spirit, a message that cries out for victory, for the power to drive our enemies before us and bring glory to Tepatiliztlan once more." Glory—but more importantly trade, the opening of ways, so that they might send out their salt and receive all the things they needed in return. In desperation her priests had prayed, and now she held the answer the gods had sent.

Her nobles shouted in approval and hope. Motzaloa rose and left the chamber, all parting before her. Attendants followed at her heels until she reached the beaded curtain that separated her private quarters from the rest of the palace. Then they fell back and stood sentry. A stronger guard than usual; Iztlacatun and Ohuiyotlan could not have heard yet about the obsidian, but they might have agents in the city who would take action on their own. The attendants guarded their lord as a matter of course, but the blade needed its own protection.

Motzaloa's hands trembled as she laid the bundle aside.

She could hear Ocachihualli outside, in the small courtyard of their quarters. His shouts rang from the stone walls, wordless, energetic cries. Motzaloa knew even before she went to look that he was practicing, lunging at imaginary enemies with his spear. His scales gleamed gold in the sun, and his quetzal feathers danced in accompaniment. Newly arrived at his full growth, still young and bursting with life.

He thought himself unobserved, and she watched him with pain in her heart. Her heir, her son, her only child. In time she might hope to bear another—perhaps. The aluxob lived short lives with abundant children; for quetzalcoameh it was the opposite. Today, in this sunlit courtyard, Ocachihualli was all she had.

Today, they were both safe. What of tomorrow, though? What of Iztlacatun and Ohuiyotlan; what of war and the threat of conquest? Tomorrow there might be no Tepatiliztlan, except as a subject city ground beneath the heel of their more powerful neighbors. Motzaloa and Ocachihualli might live for years after that, as captives of their conquerors. Brought out on the great ritual days, made to bleed time and again for the victors, a continual sacrifice to please the gods. They would not receive the mercy shown to those who gave themselves willingly, the drugs to numb the pain; for enemy nobles, suffering was part of the ceremony. Her beautiful son would live on in recurrent agony.

The god of the feathered serpents did not ask to be honored with blood. But the god of the feathered serpents was only one among many, and to save her people, Motzaloa needed more.

She watched her son without blinking, not as a mother but as the lord of Tepatiliztlan. She carved out of her heart the love she felt, the pride and fierce attachment, that would make her put this golden moment above the well-being of her city. The star of war was moving into auspicious position, Cenquiztli had told her— and now this blade came, the instrument of a great sacrifice. To save her domain, from her nobles in their shabby finery down to the alux peasants scrabbling in their fields, she must pay with treasure far more valuable than gold.

Against that, her love was nothing.

And so she sacrificed it.

Lying within the soft cotton of its final cocoon, the obsidian felt the heartbeats of all those who waited in the plaza below. People of every caste, noble and commoner alike; residents of the city; outsiders from all the villages of the domain. All those who had heard of the great sacrificial knife and were able to reach Tepatiliztlan in time, packed at the foot of the great pyramid. The stone vibrated with each beat of their hearts, their bodies pulsing like drums, filled with the precious substance that bridged the worlds of flesh and spirit.

Another drum: Ocachihualli's footsteps, climbing to the heights of the temple. Slow and careful, not only for dignity but for balance; the drink given to him numbed his senses and made movement uncertain.

Only those drums and the whisper of the breeze, scarcely dimming the punishing heat of the noonday sun. All else was silence.

A silence broken by Cenquiztli's voice, crying out prayers for the people below and the gods above. Then the faint scrape of feathers against stone as Ocachihualli bent himself backward over the rounded top of the stone. Ankle and wrist bells shimmered with soft music as four ocelotlaca held him fast, one at each limb, pinning him against the struggles he did not try to make.

The cotton fell away and the blade rose high in Motzaloa's hand.

Obsidian Butterfly: that was the name given to the goddess, of whom it was only a fragment. The personification of sacrifice, whose sharp-edged wings cut the veil between the worlds. The gods of fire and earth had sent this piece of her into the world for a purpose. Now its time had come.

It flew as it was made to do, by an artisan's hands and the cycles of the cosmos, where nothing came without cost. Out of the sunlight, sheathing itself in the body below. Blood surrounded it, hot and holy—and at last, at last, what had once been mere stone became something more.

The *axis mundi*, the point around which all things revolved. The place where life met death, where the mortal met the divine.

A few quick strokes of its sharp edge cut Ocachihualli's heart from his chest. Soon his flesh smoked in the sacred flames before the altar, bearing the prayers of the gathered people to the ears of the gods. For victory, for survival, for hope. Ocachihualli's was only the last of the sacrifices made for that prayer. The knife remembered Konil, and Jachanel, and Xamania, and Motzaloa, who stood atop the pyramid with her eyes burning dry in defiance of tears. Whether of blood or not, whether given willingly or taken by force, the price must be paid.

It was not for the knife to judge. Today it had fulfilled its purpose. Tomorrow, next year, a century from now, it would do the same, until it too was broken, becoming a precious sacrifice.

Stone was patient. Lying atop the altar in its cloak of blood, the obsidian butterfly waited, again.

Never to Behold Again

Beauty is a consumable thing. We eat it with our eyes, wear it down with our gazes. A sunset or a flower may take our breath away because we see it for so short a time; the next day the flower has wilted, and the next evening's sunset is not the one we saw before. But everyone has had the experience of purchasing a thing—a sculpture, a vase, a piece of jewelry—which was utterly striking when it was new, only to find that its charm palls after it is looked at too often. This is not simply habituation. The beauty is consumed in the looking.

I did not care about money when my daughter wed, not for its own sake. I wanted some untouched beauty.

Money is why ambitious families lock their most beautiful daughters away, to be attended to only in darkness, or by blind slaves. They choose the girls at an early age, no older than six, and they seclude them behind walls and veils until it is time for them to marry. Wealthy men will pay an absurd bride price for a young woman who has not been seen in a decade or more. Her beauty will be pristine, unmarred by other people's eyes. Of course their own greedy gazes often ruin their prizes before long, dulling the new wife's shine—but until then, they have what few others can say they possess.

That, not money, is what drove me. Through the long years in which my daughter grew unseen, I gave careful thought to my choice, considering and discarding the possibilities. By the time she married, I knew: an ink painting by the master Kilungte. His style is minimalist; each work is completed in a single sitting. Even the artist's own gaze has little chance to diminish the perfection of the result.

I looked at it once, when I received it. I stared at it without blinking, until my eyes burned so badly I could keep them open no longer. Then, with them shut, I covered the painting. And I have not looked at it since.

No one but me knows where it is. I can't risk someone else damaging it, eating away at the beauty I sacrificed so much to acquire. Perhaps I will look at it one more time before I die—I haven't decided. It will be lesser then, reduced by that first viewing. Perhaps it is better to remember it only as it was.

I will not say what the painting depicts. Words cannot suffice. It is the most beautiful thing I have ever seen, and no one will ever truly see it again.

A War of Words

Last week I had a word for it.
That feeling when something goes well,
really well,
and you're warm and bright inside—
there's a word—
but it's gone, stolen, seized in the raid;
the others have it now
in the town across the bay,
not the feeling, but yes the feeling,
and the word.

They came again this week,
with those things in their hands—
metal, sharp,
you hurt people with them,
we have them too,
but not the word—not anymore—
the sounds and the sense
taken back across the bay,
a trophy of their triumph.

Today it was the water—
the big water that divides us—
we're losing more and more,
more battles, more words,
all gone across the water I can't name anymore
because it belongs to them now,

the—
what are they—
I had a word for them this morning, I know it—

I don't know it

—I only know they'll come back
and I won't know what they've taken.
Just one thing after another
until we have no words left.

Afterword

When I first set out to organize my published short fiction into novella-sized collections, I sorted it into various categories: historical fantasy, contemporary fantasy, folklore-based stories, and so forth.

It doesn't surprise me that of the various types, the first one to get a second collection is secondary world fantasy. (In fact, though this is the first "sequel" to *Maps to Nowhere*, it's the third such collection, after *The Nine Lands*, where all the stories were set in the same world.) As I said in the Afterword to *Maps to Nowhere*, although I love playing with folklore and history, fantasy set in imaginary worlds has always felt to me like the heart of the genre, and it is certainly where my anthropology-loving spirit thrives.

It's also not surprising that three of the stories here take place in settings I've used before. Once a world has come alive in my mind, writing another tale there can feel like slipping back into a comfortable sweater, a chance to play around some more without having to create everything from scratch. And even when I've written multiple novels there—as is the case with the Memoirs of Lady Trent—there's always more to explore: even the most thoroughly detailed fictional world only scratches the surface of real complexity. So once a fresh idea comes to me, it's off to the races.

Of course, I also like doing new things. There's a great deal of freedom in being able to just *make stuff up*, without having to worry about it standing up to a novel's worth of elaboration. What would it mean for the world at large if beauty truly was diminished by observation, the way it is in "Never to Behold Again"? I don't know, and I don't have to. Which is why, although this collection has three stories piggybacking off previous work, the majority of the pieces here are entirely new.

As for that poem…I was surprised as anybody else when I started branching out into poetry. I'm not one of those people who's been writing it for years, and only recently started publishing it; poetry ambushed me out of nowhere in 2021. Relatively little of what I've written is secondary world, though, because honestly, I think that's the hardest subgenre to do in poetry: it requires *some* amount of exposition to establish the facts of the setting, and there's not a ton of space to do that in a poem. However, going in that direction does mean "A War of Words" is the first poem to be included in one of my collections, since it gets to ride along with my abundant secondary world short fiction!

And that concludes my general remarks. For commentary on the individual stories, turn the page.

Story Notes

Notes on "The Şiret Mask"

I'm not solicited for anthologies that frequently, but it does some-times happen. In this case, I was contacted by someone editing a book of stories about female rogues, asking if I would be interested in writing something in that vein?

The question came in while I was playing a con artist in a friend's tabletop role-playing game—a con artist named Ren, be-cause yes, this was the game that eventually gave rise to the Rook & Rose novels. That was not yet on the horizon, though; I just had the rogue flavor in my brain. I'd also been inspired by a blog entry (now lost to the mists of the internet) about an old silent film called *Filibus*, which features a cross-dressing, zeppelin-flying female master thief. Those mushed together in my mind, and during a weekend at a convention, this story fell out of my head in a solid piece.

…just in time for me to find out that plans had changed and the anthology had folded.

Fortunately, this story found another home right away. (On its first submission, actually.) And I had so much fun writing it that when various people said they'd happily read an entire novel about this character, I promptly came up with a concept for a whole trilogy of them! As of this collection being published, I haven't yet written those—and it'll be an odd thing in some ways if I do, because in the course of working out the trilogy idea, I wound up changing enough details that this story would be non-canonical to the series. Which will be a new situation for me; all my previous novel-related short fiction has been in continuity with the bigger picture. But better to sacrifice continuity than to confine myself to the strictures of what I wrote when the idea only had to fill a few thousand words.

I should also note something about the spelling As some of you may have noticed, the personal names here are taken from Romanian, and the place names are inspired by it. However, it was only as I was preparing this collection that I realized I'd mistakenly used the S and the t with cedillas beneath them, rather than the S and the t with diacritical commas beneath them: very similar shapes, but not the same thing! Unfortunately, I'm not able to correctly typeset the latter with the tools I use, so I'm forced to fall back on what I originally used (which, fortunately, seems to be an acceptable alternative in Romanian orthography). I wanted to state for the record, though, that I *am* now aware of the difference!

"The Șiret Mask" was originally published in issue #238 of *Beneath Ceaseless Skies*, in November 2017.

NOTES ON "AT THE SIGN OF THE CROW AND QUILL"

This story started out as a pair of earrings.

Some of you know exactly what I mean by that; the rest are scratching their heads in confusion. For the latter, I should explain that there's a well-known jeweler in the SF/F convention scene, Elise Matthesen, who routinely gives all of her pieces very interesting titles. Sometimes she'll sell those pieces to authors at a slight discount, in exchange for the author in question promising to someday write a story with the same title.

I don't know how many published works out there started life as a piece of jewelry, but this is one of them! It took me far longer to write the promised story than I originally expected, though. My first conception was that it would be some kind of highwayman tale—since the name rather suggests an old-fashioned tavern or inn—but that's more a mood and a setting than a plot, and so there it languished for many years.

I'm not even quite sure how my thoughts morphed from that into what I wound up writing, but I know it was provoked by me being invited to contribute to an anthology of "romantic fantasy"—not in the modern sense of genre romance, but in the older sense of adventure and such. I think I somehow tipped over into imagining the Crow and the Quill as people…very ominous-sounding people…something about death…hey, I like dueling… and so, in the subconscious, half-instinctive way ideas often form, this turned into the story of a very odd dueling tradition, and a chance to mess with fate.

"At the Sign of the Crow and Quill" was published in the *Lace and Blade 4* anthology, edited by Deborah J. Ross, in February 2018.

NOTES ON "DEAD MAN'S MAP"

If this story has a slightly unusual air to it, that's because it's a slightly unusual story for me.

It was written for the *Traveling Light* anthology, the brainchild of the people behind the Worldbuilding for Masochists podcast, which I've been on several times. One of the traditions of that podcast is to ask guests to contribute a new detail to an ongoing world—and with all those details built up, it seemed only natural for them to do an anthology, inviting the guests to contribute!

So "Dead Man's Map" is set in a world not of my own creation (except insofar as I contributed a few elements that don't actually appear in this story). Usually when that happens, as with my short fiction for *Legend of the Five Rings*, it's work for hire, meaning they own the copyright and I can't reprint it in any of my collections. But that wasn't the case with *Traveling Light*, and so here you go: a somewhat piratical story set in a world where teleportation gates can whisk you across the world—but, uh, without your clothing, hence this being nicknamed the world of "magical nude gates"—and the dead can be enchanted to get up and travel home for burial. Or, as you see here, they might go somewhere else…

If this intrigues you, then check out *Traveling Light*, edited by the Worldbuilding for Masochists team! "Dead Man's Map" appeared there in August 2024.

NOTES ON "ON THE IMPURITY OF DRAGON-KIND"

The internet is full of many entertaining things, and one of them is a Tumblr discussion about dragons and Jewish law, sparked by the question of whether it would be permissible to have a dragon light a fire for you on Shabbat (when observant Jews are not supposed to be doing any work such as lighting fires). This delightful conversation ranged through issues like whether the dragon is Jewish and whether it would be animal cruelty to prevent it from lighting fires, and I thought to myself, "This is exactly the kind of debate they would have for real in Lady Trent's world."

But a Tumblr discussion is not a short story; I needed a different approach. Since I wanted to keep with the principle established by the Memoirs of Lady Trent and the story "From the Editorial Page of the *Falchester Weekly Review*," that all fiction in that setting is some kind of in-world document, I started casting about for angles that would work for this. I *very* briefly entertained the notion of writing it out like a page of Talmudic commentary, with the original text at the center and accreted layers of discussion arranged around it until the whole page is packed full…but that also would not really be a story.

After talking it over with some Jewish friends, I arrived at the idea of making this a dvar Torah, a.k.a. a drash: a sermon on a passage from scripture. And to connect it to the characters, why not have it be a dvar Torah delivered by Lady Trent's son, as part of (his world's equivalent of) his bar mitzvah? I owe credit for helping me work that out and fine-tune the draft itself to fellow writer Noah Beit-Aharon.

"On the Impurity of Dragon-kind" was published in issue #29

of *Uncanny Magazine*, in July/August 2019.

Notes on "The City of the Tree"

Those of you who have read my Varekai novellas may have noticed that this takes place in the same setting: a world where supernatural creatures can be conjured into reality for an array of purposes.

I wrote this story because I'd like to do more in that world—including more with Ree, the protagonist of the novellas—but I feel like, to achieve what I want, I need a better sense of the world itself. I therefore cut myself loose from Ree herself and went exploring elsewhere, to the city where much of my larger idea will take place, with new characters and new conflicts and a new angle on how humans and archai might interact. If I have my way, you'll see more of Cahuei later, in both short stories and perhaps, someday, in a novel.

"The City of the Tree" was originally published in issue #36 of *Uncanny Magazine*, in September/October 2020.

Notes on "Silver Necklace, Golden Ring"

I almost felt like I should put this story into one of my collections themed around folkloric retellings, rather than a secondary world book. The concept started out as a retelling, and then…well. Then a lot happened.

The original seed was the Russian folktale about Koshchei the Deathless and the warrior woman Marya Morevna. For reasons I can no longer recall (except that I think they were rooted in Catherynne Valente's novel *Deathless*), I wanted to write a romantic version that paired Koshchei and Marya Morevna—but I couldn't quite get it to go.

Quite separately (at the outset), there's a detail I really love from Diana Wynne Jones' Chrestomanci novels. A central character there, Christopher Chant, has nine lives, and one of those lives winds up being placed into a gold ring for safekeeping; this eventually becomes his wife's wedding ring.

If you know the Koshchei story at all—how he's "the Deathless" because he hid his death inside a needle that's inside an egg that's inside a duck etc.—you can see how easily these two linked up in my mind.

But it still wouldn't go. Until I read Katherine Arden's Russian-based Winternight Trilogy, and also a certain Navajo Coyote story, and these things summoned thoughts of Meredith Ann Pierce's Darkangel Trilogy, and what with one thing and another, a whole lot of *vibes* cohered into what you get here: a rather twisted story that is not about Koshchei and not about Coyote and not about Christopher Chant, but which has all those things somewhere in its DNA. The result was sufficiently far from any of its roots that I decided it didn't belong among my more directly folklore-based stories, but it certainly retains that flavor.

"Silver Necklace, Golden Ring" was originally published in issue #50 of *Uncanny Magazine*, in January/February 2023. (Yes, this appears to be the collection of Stories Marie Published in *Uncanny*.)

Notes on "Chrysalis"

Oy, this story.

Alert readers may recognize the setting as being the same one that hosts "A Mask of Flesh," one of my stories in *Maps to Nowhere*. I knew when I wrote that latter piece that I wanted to do more in the setting; I had roughly three other ideas at the time, and I expected I would write them fairly soon. Fifteen years on, two of them still exist only as brief snippets and notes, but I actually wrote "Chrysalis" a mere three years later.

…and then it proceeded to sit on my hard drive, untouched and unseen, for eleven years.

The reason was the story's odd structure. The "main character"

is the piece of obsidian that gets traded from person to person; all
the other characters in the tale are there to serve its journey. Which
would be odd enough with a normal story—but this one takes
place in a setting based on Mesoamerican folklore and mythology.
So not only did I have characters passing in and out of the nar-
rative in every scene, but each one of them carried a weight of
worldbuilding baggage with them.

In short, while I liked the story, I wasn't at all sure I could sell
it.

I should have tried anyway, rather than letting doubts hamper
me. But at the time, I thought the thing to do was to write more
stories in this setting, building up a body of work that would help
familiarize readers with the setting. (Assuming they'd read the
previous stories, which is of course quite a big assumption.) So I
trunked it only *temporarily*, pending me doing more in that setting.

Eleven years later, I noticed that, uh, hadn't happened. So I
took out the draft and read through it, and while I still wondered
if I could sell it, I decided it was good enough that I ought to try.

Thus begins the second act of the saga. When Scott Andrews
of *Beneath Ceaseless Skies* read it, he (rightly) pointed out that part-
way through Motzaloa's scene, the viewpoint pulled back from
the close third it had been in up until that point, into something
more like omniscient. He suggested fixing that by breaking the
scene and shifting to Ocachihualli's perspective.

I wrote back and said, "What if I wrote from the perspective
of the rock instead?"

You see, there's a very complex structure underpinning this
whole thing. Sacrifice is such a recurrent theme in Mesoamerican
beliefs, I wanted this tale to ring the changes on the different forms
it can take: sacrifices not only of blood but of other precious things,
and sacrifices both given by oneself and taken from others, willingly and unwillingly. Over the course of the story, you get every
permutation of those three factors. Furthermore, because Mayan
mythology has the human species starting with "motherfathers"
who were both male and female, I built a gendered component
into the structure: the focus characters in the first half are both

male, and those in the second half both female, pivoting in the middle at the motherfather Cenquiztli. (Who is, by the way, the same kind of creature as Neniza in "A Mask of Flesh.")

All of this meant that no, I couldn't just switch to Ocachihualli, because that would wreck the structure. But if I added a brief scene at the very beginning to maintain the balance, I *could* use the obsidian's perspective—and in fact, doing so would help signal to the reader that the rock was, in a sense, the central character.

Actually getting that concept into a form Scott and I were both happy with took quite a few rounds of revision—our willing sacrifice of sweat! But we made it, and "Chrysalis" was originally published in issue #347 of *Beneath Ceaseless Skies*.

Notes on "Never to Behold Again"

The concept for this story got sparked when I was reading Isabel Yap's short story collection *Never Have I Ever*, which introduced me to the Filipino concept of a binukot: a young woman raised in seclusion, away from any men except family members, so as to raise her value in marriage. Such women often learn a great deal of traditional lore during those years, which I found particularly interesting.

This story isn't about a binukot, though. Instead my brain spun sideways onto the notion of young women who are prettier if nobody has looked at them—in fact, a whole philosophy or cosmology of beauty where it gets worn away by looking. That idea took a twisted and, in my opinion, rather tragic turn when I imagined someone who raised a secluded daughter entirely so they could purchase a piece of great art for themself…purchase, and then never look at again.

I'm glad we don't live in a world like the one described here.

"Never to Behold Again" was published *Daily Science Fiction*, in March 2022.

NOTES ON "A WAR OF WORDS"

In January 2024 I was reading *A Story as Sharp as a Knife: The Classical Haida Mythtellers and Their World* by Robert Bringhurst, a work that meshes selections from Haida lore with information on their history and the process by which white American researchers—one in particular, John Swanton—recorded that lore. In one of the selections, narrated by Kilxhawgins, warriors on their way to attack a village overhear the women saying "wahaaywan!," a cry of delight. They capture the women…but they also apparently capture that cry, and after that, it belongs to them.

As with "Never to Behold Again," this immediately took my thoughts in fantastical directions. What if this was a thing societies could regularly do, raiding each other to steal away words? Of course, given that it was a Native American source which sparked the idea, the allegorical implication was too obvious to miss: while colonialism has not literally carried off words as trophies, it has indeed "stolen" languages from indigenous peoples, suppressing their usage until many of them are threatened with extinction (if they're not gone already). And with the loss of language goes a loss of knowledge, culture and history and the worldview embedded in certain ways of speaking.

So while this is a speculative poem, at the same time, it's rather more pointed in its commentary on real-world dynamics than most of my writing tends to be. Based on the relatively small amount of poetry I've accumulated to date, I suspect that may be a feature of my work in that mode, that it's more willing to go directly at the theme. We shall see!

The sale of this one pleased me immensely. *Strange Horizons* has four poetry editors who work in alternating months; early in my efforts to sell them something, I happened to send my pieces in to Romie Stotz, who said such incredibly encouraging things to me that I became bound and determined that I would sell first to *that* editor and no other. Fortunately for me, that took less time and fewer attempts than my first short fiction sale to *Strange Horizons*, as detailed in the notes to *A Breviary of Fire*!

…and then, as if that weren't victory enough, it won me a Hugo Award! The Seattle Worldcon in 2025 created that as its Special Award, not only making this my first Hugo, but making *me* the first person ever to win a Hugo for poetry. Which is an absolutely gobsmacking honor.

"A War of Words" was published in *Strange Horizons* in September 2024.

About the Author

Marie Brennan is a former anthropologist and folklorist who shamelessly leans on her academic fields for inspiration. She recently misapplied her professors' hard work to *The Market of 100 Fortunes* and *The Waking of Angantyr*. She is the Hugo, Nebula, and World Fantasy Award-nominated author of the Victorian adventure series The Memoirs of Lady Trent along with several other series, over ninety short stories, several poems, and the New Worlds series of worldbuilding guides; as half of M.A. Carrick, she has written the Rook and Rose epic fantasy trilogy. For more information and social media, visit linktr.ee/swan_tower.

About Book View Café

Book View Café Publishing Cooperative (BVC) is an author-owned cooperative of professional writers, publishing in a variety of genres such as fantasy, romance, mystery, and science fiction.

BVC authors include New York Times and USA Today best-sellers; Nebula, Hugo, and Philip K. Dick Award winners; World Fantasy Award and Campbell Award nominees; and winners and nominees of many other publishing awards.

Since its debut in 2008, BVC has gained a reputation for producing high-quality e-books, and is now bringing that same quality to its print editions.

www.ingramcontent.com/pod-product-compliance
Lightning Source LLC
Chambersburg PA
CBHW030211130726

47898CB00012B/979